ALPHA ATTACKED

Big City Lycans
Book One

New York Times and USA Today Bestselling Author

Eve Langlais

1

WORKING during the full moon sucked for those in the emergency department. It wasn't just a myth that people acted a little crazier. It happened—

Every.

Single.

Time.

Unprovoked attacks. Hallucinations. And for some reason, more people came in with dog bites.

Like the others employed by the hospital, Maeve had to take her turn working the night shift on the full moon. She made her rounds, cubicle after cubicle, dealing with folks. One couple, who'd decided to bind their love in blood, needed stitches because they'd cut a little too deep. There was the guy overdosing for the second time that night who refused her offer of drug counseling. She informed three other people she wouldn't prescribe opioids and got called a few choice names. The usual stuff.

She let it all roll off her back. Addiction could be a terrible thing to deal with. Maeve's was for chocolate. Not the cheap stuff bought at the corner store. She liked her imported Belgian treats. She'd been known to get testy when Aunt Flo visited and she didn't have a piece of cocoa goodness melting in her mouth.

Around two a.m., with the moon shining super bright outside, the shit really started hitting the fan as the bars shut down, spilling the drunks into the streets. Most would stagger home or find a place to sleep it off. But others just had to cause trouble, leading to a wave of people coming into the ER. Most sported contusions and broken noses, easily triaged and gotten rid of. Those with stab wounds required a closer look.

At almost four, Maeve finally got a break. She was savoring a glorious hot chocolate with little marshmallows on top when the intercom went off.

"Dr. Friedman. Purple in R2." *Purple* was code for *gunshot wound*. Getting all too common these days with the illegal guns coming into the city. The hospital changed the color code often so that people hearing the announcements wouldn't start whipping out their phones to try to film a traumatic moment.

The macabre bent of today's society worried Maeve. Made her not regret her choice to skip having kids. Although she'd recently been thinking of getting a cat.

Seemed like a lot of responsibility when all she wanted to do when she got off shift was suck down a glass of wine while slouching on her comfy couch.

"Dr. Friedman. Code purple in R2."

She sighed at the repeated message. No more delaying. She gave her mug of chocolate, sugar heaven a mournful look and slugged back one more drink before heading at a brisk pace to the operating rooms.

Nurse Herman, also known as her best friend, Brandy, when outside of work, held open a door and gestured. "In here."

"Not R2?"

Brandy shook her head. "They switched the operating room because Jarvis is working on the lights." Jarvis being their maintenance guy.

Maeve stepped into the prep room and held out her arms as Brandy draped a clean protective suit on her. "What do we know?"

"Male. Thirties to forties. Drive-by shooting. Six gunshots, mostly to the torso."

Maeve listened to the summary as she snapped on gloves and tied a mask over her face. Just last week, she'd had to listen to some interns mocking the thin paper. Ignorant idiots. Nothing worse than sneezing on an open wound or a gusher hitting the face to appreciate the protection it afforded.

One part of Brandy's recitation caught her attention. "Did you say six gunshots, mostly to the chest?"

Brandy nodded. "It's a miracle he's still alive."

Not for long, most likely. But perhaps he'd be one of the super lucky ones.

"Have they started a transfusion yet?" she asked.

"We will as soon as we figure out his blood type. We must have gotten some faulty test strips, because the darned things keep lighting up like a Christmas tree. We sent some to the lab."

"We don't have time to wait. Get him going on O negative." The universal blood type.

"We would if we had some," Brandy grumbled. "Apparently, there's a massive shortage of it in the city."

Not the most auspicious announcement. With how much blood he'd lost and what he'd continue to lose, it would make her task of saving him darned near impossible.

Challenge accepted.

Fully suited, Maeve entered to find the patient

already stripped, a sheet over his lower half covering his groin and thighs. Nurse Abbott—a recently graduated young girl who always chirped, "Call me Ginnie"—gently sponged the chest to clean the area around the numerous oozing holes.

The monitor hooked up to him showed his heart was ticking along steadily. The blood pressure cuff on his arm inflated, providing a reading of one hundred over sixty-five. A bit low, but not dangerously so. Surprising, given the blood he must have lost.

Brandy wheeled a cart close by with the surgical tools Maeve would likely need. "Ready when you are."

"Ditto," Ginnie chirped, stepping back from the operating table.

"Where's the anesthesiologist?" Maeve asked, noting the specialist missing from his post.

"They're looking for one." Brandy sounded less than impressed as she said, "Freddy called in sick. Again."

"We have no one to put him under?" The query lifted Maeve's brows. "How am I supposed to operate?" No one had a reply. She eyed his torso and the holes. "I don't suppose the bullets went straight through?"

"Nope. Still inside." Brandy shook her head.

Meaning Maeve would have to dig. No way he'd remain unconscious. "I can't operate on him. What if he wakes up partway through?"

"He'll bleed out if you don't," Brandy pointed out.

Even if the bleeding from the wounds appeared sluggish, they had to be cleaned and sewn shut. But only after she removed any debris inside. It would involve poking and possibly some slicing. Either would likely rouse him. If he thrashed while she wielded the scalpel on his flesh, she could seriously damage something. If she did nothing, he'd probably die.

Rock, meet hard place. Rather than sigh, she took action.

"Ginnie, fetch me some lidocaine, both the swab and injection."

"Yes, Doctor." The younger nurse ran.

Maeve eyed the man. One of the wounds was shallow enough she could see the bullet. Easy to pluck. She grabbed some tweezers. "Brandy, keep an eye on him and let me know if he shows signs of waking. I'm going to start removing the foreign objects." The best she could do. If lucky, he'd remain unconscious. If not, then hopefully Ginnie would return soon with the numbing agent.

With a steady hand, she gripped the protruding

missile and pulled it free, causing the blood dammed behind it to well and roll out. A good thing, as it would help clean the wound. She poured a cleaning solution to rinse it out. "Pressure," she ordered Brandy and moved on.

Which one next? Five holes in his upper body, with a sixth missile having grazed his ribs, leaving a deep furrow.

She went after a slug wedged between the ribs, spotting it when she squirted a clear solution to dilute the blood. Amazing that it hadn't gone deeper. It clanged as she dropped it into a metal dish. The next had lodged into the muscle of his abdomen— rock-solid, she noticed, a male who kept in shape. As she wiggled the bullet from its tight hole, Brandy exclaimed, "Oh shit, he's awake."

Indeed, eyes of pale gold were open. He was aware and watching.

Like a deer caught in headlights, Maeve froze, scalpel poised over the sluggishly oozing hole.

"Don't pause on my account." He spoke in a low, smooth tone, showing no hint of pain or panic. Surprising, given the situation.

"You're awake." A dumb and obvious thing to say.

"How observant of you," he drawled.

"I'm sorry. That doesn't usually happen, but I'm

afraid we don't have an anesthesiologist at the moment to knock you out, and your situation is rather urgent."

"How many bullets?"

Brandy replied, "Six. Five inside of you. Well, two now. Three are already out."

"That would explain my discomfort." He winced and went to sit up.

Maeve immediately put her hands on him to push him down. "You can't move. We're not done extracting the bullets."

"Then, by all means, finish." He relaxed on the table and waited.

It took her a moment to sputter, "I can't. You're awake."

"Afraid you'll get stage fright?" he teased.

"No. I'm waiting for Nurse Abbott to return with lidocaine."

"I don't need any drugs. I can handle it." A big boast to make.

"You might think you can, but even the slightest flinch might cause me to slip. I can't take that chance." Maeve shook her head in refusal.

"Do it," was his soft reply.

Instead, she glanced at Brandy. "Go see where Ginnie is with that lidocaine. She should have been back by now."

"I swear if she's flirting with that new doc in oncology, I will kick her ass," Brandy threatened as she stomped off, leaving Maeve alone with the patient.

He still stared. Discomfited, Maeve looked away, asking, "How did you get shot?"

"By a gun. And just an FYI, it hurts. So fuck the waiting. Get those silver nuggets of torture out of me."

"It will just be a minute—"

"Either you do it now or I'm leaving." A baseless threat.

She snorted. "Don't be melodramatic. We both know you can't."

"I'd like to see you stop me."

She wanted to retort he was in no condition to fight off anyone. At the same time, she didn't want him exerting himself, because who knew what kind of damage he'd do? "If you'll just give my nurse a few more minutes, I'm sure she's on the way back with the freezing agent."

"And if she's not? Let's just get this done. I won't flinch. Promise." He even managed a charming smile.

Maeve poked at his wound to prove a point.

He didn't budge, but his lip lifted higher at the

corner as he drawled, "You'll have to do better than that, Doc."

"If you insist..." she mumbled. She ignored his stare to lean in close. She carefully sliced before using tweezers to pluck out the bullet that nicked his collarbone. A miracle it hadn't shattered.

He didn't even so much as gasp in pain. She eyed him after the slug plunked into the dish.

"You okay?"

"Yup."

The monitors agreed with him. His heart rate appeared to be slowing. He remained calm. Probably high as a newt. Most people who came in at this time of night were under the influence of something.

She went after the last bullet. The deepest. It had practically gone right through his shoulder. "This one would be better removed from the back. We'll flip you once my nurses get back."

"Fuck waiting. I'll roll myself over." He proceeded to remove the sensors monitoring his vitals. When he would have removed the IVs giving him fluids, she put her hand over his.

"Stop. You're being irrational. You lost a lot of blood."

"I'm fine. I don't need any of this shit." He went to yank, and once more, she grabbed at his hand.

"Wait. You'll make a mess if you pull it out like

that. Let me do it." Against her better judgment, but with little choice, given his obstinate insistence, she turned off the IV before sliding the needle out of his flesh.

The moment he was freed of all the medical equipment, he rolled to his stomach, losing the sheet in the process and baring his ass.

She must have stared a tad too long, because he snapped, "You gonna finish the job or what?"

She created an incision over the poking lump with the scalpel, and the final bullet emerged, which led to him sighing. "That's better."

"Time to sew you up." She turned to the tray to hunt for what she needed, but by the time she faced him again, he'd sat up.

"What are you doing? Lie down."

"Why?"

"Because I haven't sewn your wounds closed yet. If you strain too much, you'll lose even more blood and possibly bleed out."

He glanced down at the holes riddling his body, all of them barely leaking any blood. "I'm fine."

"You are not fine. You have five bullet holes! You've lost a lot of blood." It surprised her that he sounded so coherent.

"I appreciate the concern, Doc, but I need to get

out of here. Trust me when I say that would be best for everyone."

"You're in trouble." Stated, not asked, since it seemed quite obvious.

"What gave it away?" was his sarcastic retort.

"If someone's trying to kill you, then you should talk to the cops."

He snorted. "No, thanks."

The reply indicated a lack of trust, or perhaps a fear of the police arresting him. "If you're worried about going to jail, you could probably get a reduction in your sentence if you testify about whatever's got people using you for target practice."

That brought an incredulous look. "Snitch?"

"Because that's way worse than getting gunned down in the street."

"Listen, honey—"

"I'm not your honey. You can call me Dr. Fri—"

"Whatever. My business ain't none of yours, Doc."

"It is, given you're on my operating table."

"Then I'll remove myself." He swung his legs over the table.

She took a step back before stating, "It is my professional opinion that you require proper bandaging and monitoring for the next twenty-four hours at least."

"Think whatever you like, Doc. We're done." He hopped off the operating table and stood.

Given his nakedness, she kept her eyes on his face. "You're being a stubborn idiot. You have holes in your body. Even if you don't want stitches, then at least let me cover them. You don't want them to get infected."

"I'm pretty sturdy." He took a step in her direction, most likely because she stood in front of the door.

"You can't leave. The police will want to talk to you." The hospital had to report all gunshot wounds.

He grimaced. "Yeah, well, I ain't interested in gabbing with them."

She wanted to argue, and yet, it suddenly occurred to her how large this man was. Determined too. He towered over her, him and his many, many muscles.

She retreated a step and hit the tray of instruments, which clattered and almost tilted over. As she grabbed at it, she partially turned.

By the time she recovered, the door to the operating room was swinging shut on a bare, but very nice, ass.

Minutes later, still gaping in a room empty but for equipment and bloody sheets, Maeve blinked as Brandy returned with the long-awaited syringes.

"Took you long enough. What happened to Ginnie?"

"No idea. I didn't see her on the way to grab the lidocaine." Brandy glanced past her. "Where'd the patient go?"

"Don't know. Don't care. He wanted out, and I wasn't about to stop him." Although she did wonder how Brandy had missed seeing the oversized naked man in the hall.

"Hold on, you're saying he got up and walked out? With six bullet holes?"

"Five," she corrected. The furrow didn't count.

"Probably high on something. Wonder how long before he collapses and ends up back on the table," Brandy said.

"No table needed. The bullets are out, and in some stroke of luck, nothing vital got hit. He just needs some stitching." Which could be done by someone else. She was done for the day.

It was then that Ginnie finally returned, hands empty, brimming with excitement.

"Where have you been?" Brandy scolded.

"Sorry, had to deal with a stomach cramp."

"During an emergency?" Maeve snapped.

"It was urgent."

"You should have still contacted us. We were in the middle of surgery," Brandy said.

"By the time I was done, I got distracted by the commotion in the emergency waiting room."

Brandy muttered, "Squirrel." And it was all Maeve could do to not laugh.

Instead, she asked, "What happened?" before heading for the next room, where she could strip out of her dirty gown.

"A massive dog went bolting through the ER and out the doors."

"Someone lost their service dog?" Not a common sight to see one fleeing, given their training.

"Don't know if it was service. Doubtful, though, since I didn't see it wearing a vest."

"If it wasn't service, then how did it get inside?" The hospital didn't allow pets.

"No one knows yet. But Peabody is freaking." Peabody being one of the hospital admins.

"He should worry less about a single random dog and more about hiring another anesthesiologist. This is the second time in the last week Freddy has bailed without warning."

Freddy wouldn't be the only one she'd ask to replace. Maeve wasn't impressed that Ginnie had dallied during an emergency surgery. It could have cost the patient his life.

A patient who had disappeared. Despite his naked ass hightailing it out of the operating room, no one had seen him apparently, but everyone had heard of the dog.

After the security footage circulated, many called the dog a wolf, and no one questioned the illogic of a giant wolf running loose in the city. Par for the course on a full moon.

2

ON FOUR LEGS AND HURTING, Griffin bolted from the hospital and didn't stop running until he'd reached an alley with no prying eyes. Only then did he dare shift from his wolf to his man shape, wincing the entire time. Blame a torso riddled with bullets.

A miracle he didn't die. He would have bled out if not for the Good Samaritan who'd dragged him into his bakery, foiling the drive-by shooters. He was the one who must have called an ambulance, because a hospital was the last place Griffin would have gone. He'd have taken his chances with Ulric, who'd done a stint in the military as a field medic.

Waking during surgery? Very unexpected, as was the doctor, masked and gowned, working over him. The antiseptic smells, clashing with that of his own coppery blood, had left him disoriented. He couldn't scent the doctor, and that bothered him, since he could tell a lot by smell.

At least he'd been able to observe her calm competence as she'd leaned in and carefully plucked out the bullets. Lying still as she'd extracted them had taken all kinds of steady strength, because it had motherfucking hurt. As if he'd ever admit it. Never show weakness.

Ever.

Also, never wait for the cops.

He had no doubt if he'd stuck around waiting for her to stitch him up, they'd have appeared and asked questions he'd rather not answer.

Who shot you?

Bad people.

Why?

See above.

Who are you?

None of your fucking business.

Griffin preferred to live under the radar. No arrests. Not even a speeding ticket. A man in his position couldn't be too careful. He just hoped that when he'd fled, no one caught the fact that a man entered into a closet and a wolf emerged. He'd have to ask Dorian to check the hospital footage.

A wolf in the city wasn't an ideal disguise, but since dawn hadn't crested yet, few people had been around to see him, and those who'd briefly seen his furry, sleek shape would have assumed he was a dog. Insulting, but it worked in his favor.

Now, he ran when he could, his body weak from loss of blood and hurting too. Perhaps he should have let her stitch up the bigger wounds. He made it home without further trouble. The door on the alley, unmarked and partially rusted, the black paint peeling, opened before he could knock. The camera watching the alley would have shown his arrival.

The moment he entered, Griffin shifted, hearing the slam of the door and appreciating the blanket tossed over his shoulders.

"What the fuck happened to you?" exclaimed Quinn, who was doing nighttime security for the shop.

"I thought I'd see what target practice felt like," was Griffin's sarcastic retort. He winced as he straightened, wrapping the blanket around his waist.

He entered the main floor of the building, owned by Lanark Leaf Inc. His company. His building. His operation. All legal. Now at least. A few years ago, before the legalization of marijuana, he'd sold most of his stuff from the trunk of his car. Now he operated a few stores in the city, supplied by his country cousins who were part of the North Bay Pack. The Lanarks were now wealthy and legit. So fuck everyone who said they'd never amount to anything.

"Geezus fucking Christ, what happened to you?" The exclamation spurted from Wendell, who stood up from the table where he'd been working on the computer, running numbers. Cooking them a bit too.

Years of illegal selling had left them with some cash to launder, which they'd been doing slowly, building their bank accounts, making them healthy without doing anything crazy to draw attention. Math not being his strong suit, Griffin left the finer points of it to Wendell.

"Give me a second. I need some pants." He went for the box they kept by the back door for the times someone showed up and needed clothes. Most of the time, they didn't shift in the city. Wolves tended to draw notice. But sometimes shit happened, and when it did, they liked to be ready. Hence the box of tracksuits, all in extra large, which worked for most of the boys, except Travis, who was a foot taller than all of them, and Lonnie, who was a foot shorter. For shoes, they had garden clogs in extra large. Ugly fucking things, but cheap, and with the heel straps torn off, they fit everyone well enough until they could get home and dress properly.

The boys held off asking questions until he had some pants on. As Griffin pulled on a T-shirt that said "Don't worry, have a smoke and be happy," Wendell started.

"Who shot you?"

"Dunno." He popped his head and arms through before facing his crew, only the pair for the moment, but he had no doubt they'd already texted the others.

"What do you mean you don't fucking know? What the shit happened?"

Any other time, Griffin might have called Wendell to task for taking that tone and making that demand. But he cut the guy some slack—after all, it wasn't every day your Alpha walked in looking like a pincushion. Not to mention, Wendell had almost twenty years on him. He'd earned the right to ask questions.

"I was heading home after watching the hockey game with Phil." Phil being an old high school friend. They didn't hang out often since his wife had popped out a baby. "It finished late because of triple overtime. I was passing by Juniper's Cupcakes"— which made the best buttercream icing—"when some car slowed down and at least two people opened fire." Luckily, they were shit shots and had missed his head, or he'd not be living to tell the tale.

"Hold on, are you saying someone tried to off you?" Quinn sputtered.

"Maybe," Griffin said.

"Maybe? You're riddled with bullet holes," was Wendell's dry riposte.

"We're assuming the bullets were meant for me."

"Who the fucking else?" Wendell almost roared.

Griffin allowed it. After all, Wendell had lost his son in a shooting a few years back. A farmer had seen a wolf near his land and opened fire. They now owned that farm. As for the farmer... People called it ironic that he ended up dying in one of his own bear traps after being told by conservation authorities to get rid of them.

"You can stuff the yelling, because I don't know fuck all. I didn't recognize the car, and the folks inside it were wearing those stupid medical masks and beanies." The face coverings were left over from the COVID-19 pandemic. Not everyone had ditched them when the mandates got tossed. The police were grumbling because they enabled thieves and other lawbreakers to act with impunity since no one could identify them.

Wendell whirled back to his computer. "You said this happened by Juniper's Cupcakes?"

"Yeah. The baker's the one who actually ran outside and dragged me in to safety. Got me to the hospital where some chick doctor saved my life."

It was Quinn who offered a doubtful, "Shot six times and they let you loose already?"

"Doc didn't want to. I kind of insisted."

Wendell shook his head. "Idiot. You should have let her stitch you up."

"I wanted to leave before the cops came asking questions."

"And so what if they did? You were the one shot. You wouldn't have been in trouble."

"Better to not draw attention in the first place. Besides, the bleeding had already stopped. Once she got the silver out, they started healing."

The word *silver* had them all freezing before Wendell asked in a low voice, "They shot you with silver bullets?"

"Seems like. Sure burned like they were." In retrospect, he wished he'd grabbed the dish with the bullets, but then again, how would he have gotten it home?

"Shot with silver, and you question if you were targeted?" Wendell's tone pitched with incredulity.

"Does seem kind of coincidental." Griffin down-played it. He knew better than to have his boys get all riled up and go out looking for trouble. Better to be sure who was causing trouble before they sought revenge.

"I'll bet it's those fuckers over the river." Quinn referenced the nearest wolf pack, on the Quebec side.

"We don't know that. Why would they start shit now, given things have been working smoothly?" One of the things Griffin had done when he took over the Pack from its previous Alpha was sort shit out. Ottawa and the valley belonged to Griffin, who ran the Byward Pack, whereas the Quebec side of the Ottawa River, the Outaouais, belonged to the Sauveur Pack, run by Felix.

"I'll bet you it's those fuckers trying to encroach, because they know we've got the bigger market." Quinn shook a fist.

"Maybe. Or could be someone just wants us to think that," Griffin cautioned.

"So what are we gonna do?" Quinn cracked his knuckles, ready to lay down a beating.

"Be more careful, for starters. Until we know for sure what's going on, we should all pay more attention when we go out. That means not keeping to regular schedules. Let's make it hard for anyone to track us," Griffin suggested.

A skeptical Quinn blurted out, "How's that help us find out who shot your ass?"

"You leave that to me." He had a friend on the force, part of the Pack and yet not, given he wore the uniform. But Billy would help Griffin if he asked. "We're going to want to increase security around the shop too."

"Want me to add those cameras we were discussing on the roof?" Wendell asked. Dorian, their tech guy, had been talking about them for weeks. Currently, cameras pointed only at the front and back doors.

"Yeah. Let's do that, and make sure it catches the plates of the cars that drive by. I'll talk to Dorian about running them through a program to see if we spot repeats. He'll also be able to tell if the plates ping in the system." They had access to the licensing database for Ontario, courtesy of Dorian's cousin, who worked at the agency.

"We should also have him look to see if there's any footage of you getting shot," Wendell added.

"Excellent idea. Now that we've got a plan, I am going for a shower."

"Is that wise, given you have holes in your body?" Wendell pointed out.

Griffin rolled his eyes. "For fuck's sake, you're not my mother. I'm fine."

Only a partial lie. He left them to go up the stairs to the second floor, it and the third being his home. When he'd bought the building, right after he'd combined the three main-floor shops into one massive one for his pot business, he'd then converted the many apartments above into a single luxury home. Two floors. The first floor boasted a massive kitchen that opened onto a living room with four couches and a few chairs. He needed the space for the Pack meetings. Storage, laundry, and a bathroom rounded out the space. On the upper floor, the entire room was open, with a gym in the back corner, a lavish bathroom with no interior walls, a massive bed, another seating area, and a desk for his computer.

Stripping, he grimaced at the damage to his flesh. He'd heal, but he'd sport new scars. Not that he cared, but they would lead to questions from his bedmates he'd rather not answer. He hated them getting distracted when all he wanted to do was fuck.

Being alone, he allowed himself a hiss as the hot water hit his tender flesh. He could handle a lot of pain, more than most people. And as Alpha, even during the excruciating shift, he didn't let it show. Showing pain equaled weakness.

But he let himself feel it now, slumping under the hot spray, reliving the rapid and frightening seconds that had almost ended his life.

He should have died.

But didn't. The second mistake his attackers made.

The first? Coming after him in the first place.

3

THE DETECTIVE SHOWED up while Maeve was doing her rounds the next evening.

"Are you Dr. Friedman?"

"Yes, can I help you?" she asked absently while signing off on a patient's discharge.

"I believe you can. I was informed you were the one who operated on the gunshot victim last night?"

"Excuse me, but who are you, and why are you asking?" She glanced over her shoulder at the man, who held up a badge. A touch over six foot, with clean-cut blond hair, he wore a sports jacket over a button-up shirt and pleated trousers.

"Detective Gruff. Precinct sent me over to find out more about your patient."

"Not much to tell, Detective. He showed up in the ER presenting numerous gunshots to the body. I removed the debris. He woke in the middle of the surgery and demanded to leave. Wouldn't take no for an answer, and they don't pay me enough to argue. The end."

"Woke during?" the detective questioned.

"My fault. We didn't have the proper staff to keep him under and his life was hanging in the balance, so I had to work fast."

"Do you know his name?"

She shook her head. "No. We barely spoke."

"Did he say how he got shot?"

"Again, we only exchanged a few words, mostly me telling him to not be stupid and to let me stitch him up. About the only thing I can state with almost certainty is he is most likely involved in the drug scene."

"Why would you say that?"

"Because due to a staffing issue, we couldn't knock him out. He woke while I was removing the bullets. Didn't cry out once. Didn't even flinch when he got off that operating table. No way could anyone handle that kind of pain unless they were doped."

"Could be he's just tougher than most?"

That had her snorting. "No one is that tough."

"Did you notice anything in particular about the man? Scars? Tattoos?"

"Honestly, I was more focused on saving his life than cataloging his features. Sorry."

"If you see him again, would you give me a call?" He handed her a card, which she tucked into her pocket.

"Why the interest?"

"A man was shot. We should find out who did it."

"Given he wasn't interested in sticking around, you might want to check first to see if it's gang-related." They'd been seeing more of that kind of activity lately.

"Most likely it is, but if a war is brewing in the city, we'd like to nip it in the bud before Ottawa turns into Toronto." The violence had gotten out of control there due to lax sentencing and a focus on legal guns rather than the problematic illegal ones.

"If I were you, I'd keep an eye on the morgue. The guy left before I could stitch up his wounds or even bandage them. The chances of him not bleeding out or getting a fatal infection..." She shrugged.

"I will keep that in mind. Thank you for your time, Doctor."

"Night, Detective. Good luck finding the shooter."

The man turned to leave, only to pause and ask

casually, "I hear there was a wolf on the loose in the halls last night."

She snorted. "We don't get wolves in the city, just people mistaking large dogs for them because of the full moon."

His lips twitched. "That does tend to ensure things can get pretty hairy. Thank you."

The night passed without anything exciting other than the usual—people vomiting because they ate bad food, appendixes exploding, and accidents involving power tools, which she never understood. Like, who decided using a table saw at three a.m. was a good idea? She looked forward to a relaxing three days off after eight straight night shifts.

Brandy spent their fifteen minute break talking about the handsome detective and seemed inordinately pleased he'd written his cell phone number on the back of his business card. *"In case I need to contact him,"* Brandy added with a pleased smile. Maeve didn't point out he most likely meant about the case.

She headed to her car, her mouth watering in anticipation of a glass of wine. She couldn't wait for that warm glow, coupled with reading a few chapters of a book. As she neared her spot in the employees' parking lot, she noticed someone leaning against her bumper. She'd slowed and pulled out her phone, ready to dial 911, when the man lifted his head. She blamed the new parking lot lights for the way his eyes gleamed, shining like those of an animal. The lower half of his face was covered by a neck gaiter.

Rather than confront him, because only an idiot would do that by herself in a parking lot at the ungodly hour of six a.m., she whirled around and walked quickly toward the hospital, only to falter as someone stepped out in front of her. A different guy, scruffy and dressed almost identically to the guy by her car, in leathers. His face covering resembled a skull.

She held up her phone. "Don't come any close. I'm calling 911." Actually, she'd dialed hospital security, given they were closer.

"Are you Dr. Friedman?"

Hearing her name sent a chill through her. She whirled toward the first guy as he approached. "Who are you? What do you want?"

"Where's the box?"

"What box?" she asked in genuine confusion.

"Don't play dumb. Lawyer said he shipped it to one Dr. Friedman in Ottawa."

"I'm sorry, but you have the wrong person. I haven't received any packages, nor am I expecting any. Have you checked the tracking for your parcel?"

She remained calm as she sought to divert the odd line of accusation.

"He sent it special delivery. By accident, and now we're looking to get it back."

"I'm sorry, but I can't help you."

The man cocked his head. "You better not be lying."

"I have no interest in receiving any kind of package associated with the type of people who think it is okay to accost a person in a parking lot." She couldn't help the rebuke. In plain sight of the hospital, her place of work, she was being harassed over something she had nothing to do with. She just wanted to go home, darn it.

"Aren't you the hoity-toity bitch? Think being a doctor makes you better than us?"

"I save lives. Can you say the same?" As dawn lightened the sky, her bravery grew. This area would soon get busy.

"World's got too many people, if you ask me," the first accoster stated, hooking his thumbs in his belt loops. "When was the last time you talked to Theodore Russell?"

"Excuse me?" she exclaimed, not having to fake her confusion.

"Theodore Russell. Your dad. When was the last time you heard from him?"

"Never met him." He'd left when she was little.

"Ask her if she's the one who saved the mutt last night," the other man asked in a nasally voice.

"I save lots of lives." The most honest reply.

"This fellow should have died, given he had quite a few holes in him." The fellow in front held up his hand and mimed shooting a gun. Her blood ran cold.

"Are you the one who gunned him down?"

"With a little bit of help from my friends." A chilling reply.

Rustling movement had her whipping her head to see Scruffy and yet another fellow flanking her. Each of the three hid his face.

Not good.

"You need to leave right now. The police are on their way," she said loudly, hoping whoever answered her call in security got the hint.

"We ain't gonna hurt you, not today. But we will give you a friendly warning. Next time that fucker or one of his mangy Pack comes into your emergency room, they better not leave it unless it's in a body bag. Do I make myself clear?"

"I am not letting someone die on my table because you've got a problem with them."

"Then I guess I better make sure we don't miss

next time." She could only imagine the evil grin to match his tone.

"Hey, you, what are you doing harassing our staff?"

Maeve could have slumped in relief as Benedict came jogging into sight, hand on his holster.

"Let's go, boys," stated the man in charge, but before he followed his friends, he offered a parting shot to Maeve. "If you do end up receiving a box, drop it at the Grendell. And don't even think about keeping it, or next time, maybe you'll be the one with a few holes in your body."

The fellow took off with his friends as the elderly Benedict arrived at her side, huffing. "You okay, Dr. Friedman?"

Barely. But she nodded and replied, "I'm fine. Thanks for coming to the rescue."

"No problem. Fucking druggies. We'll have to step up the patrols. Can't have the staff being harassed."

She didn't correct the misassumption. Mostly because the threat made no sense. Why would anyone think she could be involved in anything illicit? Because she had no doubt that whatever this box they wanted contained, it had to be against some kind of law. Not to mention, who but a thug would threaten a doctor and order her to ignore her oath?

When someone came into the hospital, how they got there and why didn't matter. She was duty-bound to do everything in her power to save their life.

Which reminded her of the detective. She really should contact him and tell him what had just happened. Going down to the station, giving a statement, answering questions and probably looking at mug shots would take hours.

Sigh. The sky kept brightening, which only highlighted her fatigue. And for what? She didn't want to get involved. This was a case of mistaken identity. She wasn't in possession of a box.

Benedict walked Maeve to her car. She drove straight home and used the garage door opener to slide right in, watching her rearview as the door shut, suddenly paranoid about someone getting in. She shed her jacket, purse, and shoes, putting the latter in the rubber tray by the front door. She almost fell over when the doorbell rang.

A voice chimed from her house hub, "Someone's at the front door."

Rather than open it, she moved to the window for a peek. A delivery truck was parked out front, and its driver was already heading away from the house. Hands empty. As he drove off, she opened the door to find a box with no other markings than the handwritten address on top, with her name.

M. Friedman.

For a second, she flashed to those guys in the parking lot. Suddenly afraid, she dragged the box inside and locked the door. Leaning against the door, she stared at the box.

Could be a coincidence.

Wine. Wine would fix this. Her hands trembled as she worked the cork out of a bottle of sauvignon blanc.

She downed it as she walked around the box she'd placed in her living room. The curtains were drawn over the windows, as if she feared someone spying.

Ridiculous. This neighborhood was safe. Although she really should look at getting the alarm system fixed. Three of the window sensors needed replacing.

As she sipped from her second glass, she fetched a knife and sliced through the tape holding the flaps of the box closed. Lifting them, she found a second box inside and an envelope addressed to her, embossed in the top left corner with the name of a law firm.

Okay, this was getting weird. Sipping wine, she held the envelope in her hand and eyed the box within a box. The second one appeared to be of the kind seen in law offices—cardboard with a lid and handles. A lift and a peek showed folders and other stuff. Atop all that sat a folded, lined sheet of paper.

Light-headed suddenly, she dropped the lid and took more sips of wine before she opened the envelope from the law office. Inside was a typed letter. The gist? Her deadbeat dad was dead. And his things were in the box.

Oh hell no. As if she cared if the man who'd donated sperm to make her had died. She didn't know him, and she had no interest in starting now.

She grabbed the box and marched to the front door, ready to toss it outside. Only to pause. What if she later regretted getting rid of it? Of losing her chance at finding out more about her dead-beat dad. Perhaps she should wait a bit until she'd had a chance to think it over.

She tucked it away in her basement. Out of sight. Out of mind.

The glass of wine she downed didn't cure the trembling in her hands, and she had the hardest time falling asleep. When she did finally slip into a restless slumber, nightmares of monsters chasing her ensured she felt worse when she woke.

As she sipped on a coffee, which really needed to be administered intravenously, she called Brandy. "I am not going to be able to make that movie tonight. I am exhausted. Couldn't sleep."

"I heard you got accosted in the parking lot."

"Who told you?"

Brandy snorted. "Benedict told Darcy, who told everyone."

"It was scary." She didn't mention the box or her dad. "Benedict said he'd ask for more security."

"And he'll be told no because Peabody is a tightwad."

"I'm sure we don't have to worry. Those guys mostly wanted to give me a warning."

"About?"

"Basically, I should have let Mr. Gunshot Victim die. Apparently, he wasn't supposed to walk out on his own two feet."

"Oooh, that's juicy." Maeve could almost imagine Brandy's rounded eyes as she gushed, "I wonder why they want him dead."

"Don't know. Don't care."

"You obviously care, otherwise you would have slept," astute Brandy pointed out. "Get dressed."

"Why? I just told you I am not in the mood for a movie."

"I heard that part. And that's not why I'm coming to pick you up. You need to relax, and lucky for you, I know just the place to help with that. Lanark Leaf. A pot shop."

4

GRIFFIN STOOD by the big window of his apartment while Billy relayed all he'd found out about his shooting.

"I've yet to confirm it, but hospital security filed a report about a doctor being harassed in the parking lot after her shift."

"And this pertains to me how?" he asked, turning from the window.

"It might not, but I thought it was interesting that three guys in masks appeared to specifically target the same doctor that took care of you."

That got his attention. "Did she say what they were after?"

Billy shook his head. "The report didn't say, and I haven't talked to her yet. She's not working until

Tuesday, and while I have her address, I don't think I should visit her at home about it. Technically, this isn't an official case. If she were to call the precinct—"

Slashing a hand through the air, Griffin cut him off. "Don't do anything that would draw attention. I'll handle it."

"Are you sure that's wise?"

"Gotta do something. The boys are restless. They want blood for what happened." In the Pack, loyalty proved fierce. They would die for one another.

"I don't know if the incident with the doctor and your shooting are connected."

"Guess I'll soon find out. What's her address?"

"I'll text it to you."

Griffin rubbed his bristly jaw. "Do you think it might have been the Sauveur Pack?" Their rivals from across the river.

"My contact inside is claiming it wasn't them."

"As if they'd admit it," Griffin grumbled. At the same time, this didn't feel like something Felix, the rival Pack leader, would do. "I take it you still haven't found any security footage from the area?" The shooting had happened fast, and Griffin hadn't seen much more than the blur of a moving vehicle and muzzle flashes.

"Nope. And even if we did, I'll wager whatever car they drove was either missing its plates or stolen. Could even be the one they found burned to a crisp under an overpass this morning."

"So what you're saying is we have fuck all." Griffin sighed.

"Sorry, boss. I'll keep digging."

"Don't apologize. This ain't your fault. I appreciate everything you do. But be careful. Anyone willing to come after me won't hesitate to kill you."

"They can try." Billy offered a cocky grin.

"Be careful."

"You're the one who needs to watch out. We can't have you dying on the Pack and leaving a vacuum in the leadership. Then we just might get stuck with Felix and his strange predilection for protein shakes."

"Gee, I feel so loved."

"Would you rather I blew smoke up your ass?"

"Yes!" Griffin grumbled with a grin. "You should get going before anyone catches you with me."

While Billy belonged to the Pack, outsiders didn't know that, and they wanted to keep it that way. That meant not letting anyone outside the boys see Griffin and Billy together. Part of the reason he'd bought this building was because of its secret subterranean access. A previous owner had not only built a hidden staircase that had concealed doors on each floor but they'd also literally carved an access tunnel from the basement to the subway system. It made sneaking in and out of the place easy, especially since only the Pack knew of the secret passages.

As Billy headed for the fake panel hiding the topmost door, he paused by the row of security monitors, the screens featuring video from various cameras placed around the shop. Billy pointed. "Looks like the doctor knows who you are."

"What's that supposed to mean?"

"Because that's her in your shop, browsing the vapes."

With that surprise announcement, Billy left, and no surprise, Griffin wanted a peek at the doctor. He stared at the screen and cataloged the woman. She was a real beauty, which he'd not realized, given only her eyes had been visible during their first meeting. He'd also been understandably distracted by his many bullet holes.

She had long dark hair pulled into a messy bun, fine features, full lips, and, in those hip-hugging jeans, the kind of body to make a man take more than a second look. Hot. Probably taken. *A shame*, was all he could think as she bent over a display case to look at something that the woman beside her pointed out.

Why had she come to his store? Could be a coincidence. After all, even doctors smoked pot. However, with the secret Griffin kept, he never assumed anything.

What if the doctor had somehow recognized him? Had she been to his shop before and maybe seen him working the counter? Not something he did often, not anymore at any rate. Had she hunted him down, and, if yes, why? He didn't recall doing anything in the ER where anyone could see. The moment he'd fled the operating room, he'd entered an empty room to shift. He'd given a good sniff to ensure no one was nearby before he'd exited into an empty hall. Once he'd gotten out of that section, he hadn't been able to avoid notice. People had seen a wolf, yes, but none should have associated it with a patient escaping the ER.

But what about before he'd regained consciousness? Could be the doctor had seen something suspicious. What of those men in the parking lot? Had they put her up to visiting his shop?

Curiosity had him throwing on a zippered hoodie to which he added a ball cap and shades. It wouldn't fool anyone from the Pack who sniffed him, but for anyone casually glancing in his direction, he'd be fairly anonymous. He headed downstairs and slipped into the storage room, listening as the doctor and her friend chatted with Lonnie at the register. A processed sale resulted in a beep. His signal to go.

Griffin skulked in the alley before the main door to the shop chimed their exit. He counted to ten, knowing how long it would take them to pass this spot. If he didn't see them, then that meant they'd gone the other way.

At seven, they passed by, a pair of friends unconcerned about the world. They never even noticed him slipping behind them, just another pedestrian out walking on a nice Saturday afternoon. They didn't go too far, turning onto a side street that held older residential housing—two-story buildings, rectangular in shape and bricked, a style that peppered much of Ottawa.

When they turned up a sidewalk to a home, he kept going on the opposite sidewalk, not turning back to look until he heard the slam of a door. Only then did he cross and backtrack, slipping into the backyard of a home two doors up from it. The For Sale sign out front and the lack of curtains on the windows made it a good place to hide out and watch. Once he got inside, of course. Not hard when the lockbox had individual keys that held the scent of whoever pressed them on each visit. It just took figuring out the order. In no time, he was inside and headed to the top floor, where he cracked a window and kept watch on the house with the doctor and her friend inside. The doctor's home? He'd soon find out.

He fired off a message to Billy.

Hey, what's that doctor's address?

As he waited for a reply, it occurred to him that he still didn't know her name. But he might know how to find out. He pulled up the hospital website on his phone. Within a few clicks, he was going through the list of doctors on staff. All names, no pictures.

Luckily, Billy messaged him with everything he needed.

Maeve Friedman.

Current address was the house he'd shadowed her to. Thirty-seven years old. No crimes on file. Not even a speeding ticket.

Her name, location, and knowing what she looked like were enough for him to locate her on social media. While she didn't post much, her profiles indicated she was single.

Given Griffin had a few hours until nightfall, he napped, his body needing it after the trauma. Rapid healing, a Lycan attribute, took a lot out of him.

When he woke, night had fallen and the streetlights had come on, enough to illuminate the area while also creating deep pockets of shadow. Perfect for skulking. He left the house via the back and carefully made his way over, weaving through the small yards, hoping no one spotted him and called the cops.

When he reached the doctor's property, he dropped down to inspect the bars on the basement windows. Rusted in place. He wouldn't be getting in through there.

He eyed the back of the house, with its sliding glass door and a small patio with steps leading down to the scrap of a yard covered in pebbles. The yuppie way of avoiding having to cut grass.

The sudden whoosh of the sliding door had him ducking out of sight, tucking against the porch, hoping whoever stepped out didn't glance down. A scent drifted to him, soft, with a hint of vanilla and soap. Was it the doctor? He'd been out of it in the hospital, his senses not fully functioning, not to mention she'd been sterilized before working on him.

A board creaked as she moved to the edge of the deck. He heard her inhale before he smelled the blowing smoke from the vape. Sweet, with a hint of skunk. Probably a nighttime blend. Very popular with the white-collar folk.

A quick peek confirmed the doctor was the one smoking. She took about three tokes before heading back in. *Click*. The lock engaged. Smart. In the city, you could never be too careful. His shop had bars over the windows and reinforced steel doors.

But as cautious as people were about access points on ground floors, they tended to pay less attention to windows on second floors. He glanced up. The back porch had no awning. At the front, though, he recalled the covered front step. Well lit. He needed another way to get up and in.

He returned to the house he'd napped in, this time using the window on the second floor to climb out and onto the roof. City living meant close proximity. It was all too easy for him to cross over to the next house and then the doctor's. The next part proved trickier, as it required him finding an unlocked window, then balancing on the ledge outside of it, popping the screen—quietly, of course— then sliding open the glass pane. He wiggled into a room that could only be hers. The scent of the doctor permeated it.

He didn't turn on a light but could see well enough in the dim shadows. A bed with only one big pillow, the covers pulled taut. A nightstand on either side. A dresser at the foot. Sliding mirrored doors for the closet. A single door out. Older homes like this one didn't have the all but customary master bath.

He crept across the room for a peek out the door,

only to duck back in when he heard the creak of someone coming up the stairs.

Where to hide? The closet door would make noise with its old metal track. Escaping via the window would take more time than he had. He dove under the bed, hoping the ruffled skirt didn't waver for too long.

She entered, flicking on a switch. Under the bed, his view impeded by the filmy fabric, he could get only a vague impression of feet and ankles as she moved around the bedroom. He heard the rustles as she sloughed her garments and dropped them into a bin, followed by the open-and-close slide of a drawer as she pulled out pajamas. The sexy, slinky version or the practical kind?

Not that it mattered. The light went out, and she padded to the bed, the box spring creaking slightly as she got in.

Well, fuck. There would be no moving until she fell asleep.

As he lay under her bed, waiting, it finally occurred to him to ask himself, *What am I doing?*

He honestly wasn't sure why he'd felt the need to come inside. What exactly had he expected to find? She didn't work with his enemy, obviously, or she would have let him die in the ER.

But she'd been in his shop.

Buying dope. The best in the city.

Which she'd then smoked.

He was such an idiot. A paranoid one who was currently stuck under a bed as the woman in it tossed and turned, restless, bothered by something.

Unlike Griffin. He ended up falling asleep before she did.

5

EVENTUALLY, the pot, mixed with her exhaustion, did the trick and Maeve fell asleep, drooling onto her pillow until the sound of breaking glass woke her.

Startled, she stiffened in bed. Had she imagined hearing something? Dreamed it? She rolled over, the groan of her mattress and rustle of her sheets loud in the silence. When she stilled in her new position, she strained to listen.

Heard nothing.

She snuggled her pillow.

Creak.

Her eyes shot open. That sounded like someone coming up the stairs. The third step always made a noise, no matter where you put your weight.

She sat up and reached for the baseball bat she kept by the bed. She'd seen too many gunshot victims to ever own a firearm herself. Gripping the aluminum slugger, she swung her legs over the side of her bed and stood. She held it one-handed and ignored her phone on the nightstand. She didn't want to call for help precipitously. If this was an emergency, she just had to say *Tweedle-dee* to have the macro she'd programmed into her home hub call 911. A safety class she'd taken had advised against using common words so they wouldn't trigger an emergency response by accident.

She inched toward the open door to her room, only to pause as she heard a thump. Then another, followed by a grunt loud enough to raise her brows. She slammed her bedroom door shut and shouted, "Tweedle-dee!" She ran for the phone, really wishing she hadn't dragged her heels about fixing her alarm system.

Her phone finished dialing as she snagged it one-handed.

It rang once and was answered. "911, what's your emergency?"

"Someone broke into my house, and they're still here!" The normally unflappable Maeve was disturbed. Knowing crime happened and having it happen to her were two different things, the latter being frightening. On the advice of the 911 operator, she remained in her room, clutching the bat, listening to the soothing voice keeping her updated on the progress of police.

When she heard the pounding on her door and received confirmation cops stood on the other side, she ventured into the hall, clutching her phone and bat. The door being kicked open led to her wincing. At the shouted, "Hands up!" she lifted them.

"Drop your weapon!" screamed an officer, aiming his gun at her.

Her eyes widened. She dropped the bat, which clunked hard and startled the young law enforcement officer.

It took a barked, "What the fuck are you doing, Peterson? Holster your fucking weapon," before the rookie lowered the gun.

She could have sighed in relief at the sight of the familiar man walking into view at the bottom of the stairs.

"Detective Gruff," she exclaimed happily.

"Dr. Friedman, are you okay? I heard on the squawker you had a break-in."

"I'm okay." She came down the steps, hearing the creak of the third one from the bottom.

"Did you see anything?"

She shook her head. "I hid in my room."

"Smartest thing you could do." The detective pointed in the direction of her living room. "Looks like they came through your front window. Made a bit of a mess too."

"Where are they?" She clutched her phone with both hands.

"That's what we're trying to figure out. First, we'll make sure they're not still inside. Peterson, check upstairs. O'Connor, you do the basement. I'll stay with the doctor and keep an eye on the main floor."

As the two officers in uniform scattered, she eyed the detective. "I'm surprised they sent you."

"I happened to hear your name come over the scanner and thought I'd pop over to make sure you were okay."

"Like I said, I hid. I'm fine." Technically. She'd sustained no injury other than to her mental state.

The detective moved to the living room and took in the mess, from the shattered glass littering the floor to the toppled plant stand and side table. "Doesn't look like they were being too quiet. Most likely a druggie looking for petty cash or stuff to fleece."

"Sounded like people fighting." She'd heard grunting and a thud, as if a fist had met flesh. Then again, she'd listened for only a second before shutting herself away in her bedroom.

"Maybe there was more than one and they got in a tiff."

"Maybe." She hugged herself somewhat skeptically. Especially since it didn't make her feel any better.

Peterson reappeared. "Upstairs is clear."

O'Connor followed immediately, parroting the same about the basement.

The detective waved a hand. "Clear this level then hit the yard."

The officers went off, and she asked, "Do you think they're still here?"

"Nope, but best to make sure."

"You really think it was someone looking for drug money?" She gnawed her lower lip.

"Most likely, unless you think they were looking for something else?"

For a second, her mind flashed to the guys in the parking lot, the ones who'd wanted a box. Could it be related? A chilling thought, as it meant they knew where she lived.

Before she could say anything, Peterson returned. "No one here."

"Where's O'Connor?"

"In the yard, checking between the houses."

"Seems as if the house thieves have fled. I doubt they'll be back, but you might want to sleep elsewhere until you get that window fixed. If you've got any plywood kicking around and a drill, I can help you cover it up."

"I usually hire people to fix those kinds of things."

That led to Detective Gruff putting his hands on his hips. "We can't leave you alone with a broken window. It's like an invitation to the malfeasants. Peterson, stay with the doctor. I'll be right back."

"Wait, what's going on? Where are you going?"

Turned out he wasn't gone long and hadn't gone far, because he soon returned with a wooden pallet and a drill. The detective had Peterson help him pull the pallet apart and then hold it in place while he screwed it to the window frame.

He secured Maeve's home, and when he was done, he smiled and said, "No one's getting in through there."

"Thanks."

She meant it. He'd done his best to make her safe, and yet, once the detective and the officers left, she couldn't go back to sleep. Instead, she sat in the dark on her couch, bat across her lap, wondering when her life had gotten so complicated.

6

GRIFFIN POPPED up in Billy's back seat as he pulled away from the doctor's house.

The detective flicked him a glance in the rearview. "I can't believe you were in her house."

"Guess you smelled me." He grimaced. The problem with dealing with others of his kind.

"Yes, I fucking smelled you. You're lucky she didn't. What were you doing in her house?"

"Checking her out. I got caught inside and had to lie low, waiting for an opportunity to leave." A long, roundabout explanation that avoided admitting he'd fallen asleep.

"What if she'd seen you?"

"She didn't, and it turned out it was a good thing I chose tonight to spy, given what happened."

"You took a big chance just to save her from a robbery."

"Was it only a robbery?" Griffin asked.

"Seems most likely. This street might be gentrified, but you and I both know a few blocks away is a haven for petty criminals." Low-income housing didn't always go to the neediest. The dregs always knew how to weasel in, paving the way for violence and theft.

"Guess we'll find out the motive when we question him."

Billy slammed on his brakes. "Hold on a second. You caught the guy who broke in?"

"Yeah. Although he didn't go quietly. Didn't help she's got the squeakiest fucking stairs. He heard me coming down. I'll have to remember for the next time."

"Next time?" Billy turned to ogle him directly. "You shouldn't have been inside her house in the first place."

A good point that he didn't quite have an answer for. "Maybe. Or could be Lady Luck smiled at me and put me in the right place at the right time."

"Sounds more like you're trying to make a simple B&E into more than it is."

"Why do you keep assuming it was random?"

"Did the guy you capture say anything?"

"Nope. I hit him a little hard. When he wakes up, we'll talk to him."

"I'm surprised you left him behind. What, did you stash him in the bushes?"

"Your trunk, actually."

Billy leaned his head on the steering wheel. "Are you fucking kidding me? What if someone saw you heaving his body into my trunk?"

"No one saw. Thanks for parking in a dark spot. Besides, you and I know all eyes were on the flashing lights."

"And if I'd not shown up, what would you have done?"

"Handled it." The empty house and its stone-block basement would have worked fine for his questioning tactics.

"You're acting uncharacteristically crazy."

"Am I? The guy in your trunk, he's Lycan."

That had Billy frowning. "Are you sure? I didn't smell anyone other than you, the officers, and her inside."

"Because his clothes are doused in something masking his scent. But trust me when I say he's wolf. Meaning this likely has to do with the Pack."

"Why go after the doctor?"

"As a warning to me because she saved my life?" Griffin shrugged. "I'll admit, going after her makes no sense, which is why I have questions for our guest in the trunk. Can you drop us outside the city?"

"Not planning on letting him live?"

"You know how I feel about crime." Griffin fucking hated thieves who preyed on the weak. And hated even more thugs who hurt people for no reason. An ironic stance, some would say, from a drug dealer.

"Just a regular superhero," Billy drawled.

"You're one to talk, *Detective*."

"You know we have something we call a justice system."

"Which takes too long, sentences are too light, and the whole process costs the taxpayers a fortune, especially with career criminals. My way is much more efficient."

"And risky."

"Our entire existence is risky, so it might as well be meaningful."

Billy shook his head. "One of these days, I might not be able to cover for you."

"Understood. And if I'm that sloppy, then I'll deserve it."

Because he wasn't about to stop, or tell the boys to stop, quietly cleaning up the streets of Ottawa. No one cared about the missing thugs or the crack addicts who stole purses or broke into cars. Taking care of rapists meant sparing their victims from reliving the trauma in court. Something he felt strongly about, considering what his older sister, Allie, had gone through as a teen. One of the first things he'd done when he'd turned Lycan? Hunt that raping fucker down to make sure he never hurt anyone's mother, sister, or daughter again.

"So did you find out anything interesting about the doctor while you were spying?" Billy asked, pulling back onto the road.

"Nothing. Seems like a regular working broad with a love of vanilla scents."

"She's good-looking."

A harmless statement by Billy, and yet, Griffin found himself growling. "Stay away."

That led to Billy arching a brow. "So it's like that?"

"Like what?"

"You're interested in her."

"No." A vehement denial.

"If you say so, boss." Billy made no attempt to hide his mirth.

As they thumped over an overpass, a light on the dash pinged, and Billy exclaimed, "The trunk's open."

He slammed on the brakes as Griffin piled out of the car. But it was too late. The man he'd captured had escaped and leaped over the rail of the overpass, plunging to the highway below. He didn't survive the jump.

Griffin stared down at the splayed body and the car that had swerved to a stop to avoid hitting him. Billy joined him at the rail and murmured, "What the fuck is going on?"

"No idea."

But anyone who would rather kill himself than answer questions indicated something big.

And Griffin meant to get to the bottom of it.

7

Maeve's window got fixed on Monday, and despite her trepidation, she didn't have bars placed over it and the rest of her windows. She'd lived in the house for almost a decade, and this was the first break-in. Statistically, she should be good for a while. That didn't help her nerves any.

When she returned to work on Tuesday for a day-shift rotation, she found the busy schedule of treating patient after patient did much to calm her anxiety. No emergency surgery with a handsome man waking up in the middle. No masked thugs threatening her for daring to do her job and saving a life. No demands to hand over a box that she never asked for nor wanted. A box she really should just kick to the curb.

Just a normal day, yet as her shift ended late in

the afternoon, with twilight falling, her nerves tightened. Jeff, the security guard by the main entrance, smiled as she approached. "Evening, Dr. Friedman."

"Hello, Jeff. I don't suppose I could get an escort to my car."

"Heard what happened to you the other night. Fucking junkies." He shook his head. "Just give me a second. Got to log out and lock my station." Jeff sat in a booth to monitor pedestrian traffic in and out of the hospital, dealing with any problems that arose. In a hospital, things could escalate in seconds, as people in pain, whether physically or emotionally, could lash out at any time.

"Appreciate it," Maeve said even as she disliked this new anxiety in her life.

Brandy seemed to think she'd get over it. *Give it a few weeks, and you'll forget all about it.*

Maeve sure as heck hoped so.

While Jeff finished locking the door to his cubicle, the shouting started. A glance at the lobby of blue bucket chairs showed two men shoving each other.

"Sorry, Doctor," the security guard said. "I need to deal with this first."

"Of course." Maeve watched him hurry to break up the fight, only to wince as Jeff caught a stray punch to the jaw.

The guard shook his head and then pointed his finger at the men. "Out!"

"But—"

Now they started arguing about how, despite causing trouble and then hitting Jeff, they weren't to blame. From past experience, Maeve knew this wouldn't be resolved quickly. She eyed the main doors and the stream of people passing through. Barely dark outside and still busy. She'd be fine.

Shoulders back. Deep breath. She strutted out the front doors and marched quickly to the parking lot. The staff had their own well-lit gated area, and yet, her gaze flitted from side to side. She was nervous and jerked at any perceived movement.

As she neared her car, she clutched her keys, one protruding from her knuckles as she'd been taught in self-defense class. She clicked the locks. The taillights flashed, illuminating a slumped shape skulking between her vehicle and the next. The person straightened.

Not again.

She halted and would have turned to run, except the waiting man pulled back the hood of his sweatshirt, showing his features. No mask, so she recognized him. As if she'd forget the square jaw of the gunshot victim who'd walked out the other night.

Had she not pulled out the bullets herself,

she would have never known he'd been injured. He strode confidently in her direction. Probably still high. No one had that kind of pain tolerance.

And if he was here, in this parking lot, it could be for only one thing. More drugs.

She held up her hand in warning. "Stop right there. Don't take another step."

He stilled. "Hello again, honey."

"I'm not your honey. Why are you here? What do you want? I don't carry drugs with me, nor can I prescribe any."

"Geezus, do folks really accost you for that kind of shit?" He sounded surprised.

"Addicts have no boundaries. I guess I should also mention I never carry cash."

He grimaced. "Not a thief. Or an addict, for that matter."

"Claims the man accosting me in the parking lot." Maeve didn't let down her guard for one minute, no matter how coherent he sounded.

He arched a brow. "Hardly accosting, given we're, like, six feet apart."

"This parking lot is for employees only. You shouldn't be here."

"I want to talk to you."

"And thought it was a good idea to stalk me

outside instead of coming into the hospital, where you wouldn't appear so threatening?"

His lips twisted. "Guess I didn't think it through. But I can assure you I'm not here to cause any harm."

"Then why are you here?"

"Couple of reasons. Firstly, it occurred to me I was an asshole the other day. There you were, fixing me up, and I gave you grief. Sorry about that." The apology emerged in a low drawl and sounded sincere.

"Don't worry about it. People say lots of stuff when they're in pain." In that vein, she angled her head and asked, "How are the wounds doing?"

"Good. They're healing."

"Have you been keeping an eye out for infection?"

The corner of his mouth lifted. "I'm fine, but if you'd like to check for yourself, say the word, and I'll strip."

Was he seriously flirting? "You've apologized. Now, if you don't mind, I'd like to get home. It's been a long day."

"Understood, but that's not the only reason I want to speak with you. I gotta know—does the name Theodore Russell mean anything to you?"

She froze. Why suddenly all this interest in her father? "Why?" A cagey reply.

"It's a yes-or-no answer, honey."

A purse of her lips went with her low, "I know the name."

"Doesn't sound as if you like the guy."

"I hate him." A vehement reply.

"Seems kind of harsh. Theodore Russell is your father." Stated, not asked.

"I have no father."

"Not according to your birth record."

"You hacked my personal files? How dare you?" The invasion shocked.

"Hardly hacked. The information kind of landed in my lap, and I verified it."

The admission did nothing to ease her mind. "Who are you? Why are you snooping into my life?"

"Because you're related to Theo Russell, which only partially explains what they're doing here," he muttered.

"Who's doing what here? And why are you interested in my dead father?"

"So you are aware of his death. Given your dislike of him, I am going to guess you weren't close."

"Can't be close to someone I've never met. He skipped out on my mom when I was a baby."

"And never visited?" A surprise lilt entered his query.

"Nope."

"Surprising since he never missed a monthly support payment."

She frowned. "Excuse me? My father never gave my mom a cent." Her mom used to bitch all the time about the bastard who'd shirked his duty.

"Oh, he did pay, and generously too. His lawyer kept all the receipts."

"Liar. That kind of stuff would be confidential."

"Usually, yes, but the situation is special, which is how I know he paid for your braces, your first car, and medical school."

Her spine stiffened. "My mom did all that. My father was a deadbeat who left us and never had anything to do with me."

"Bank statements don't lie." The implication being her mother had.

"My mom would have told me." A weak rebuttal.

"I'm sure she had her reasons and it's probably tied into why your father never came to see you in person. But on the flip side, he never shirked his financial responsibility to you. I can prove it if you want."

She blinked at him. "No point, because I don't care." She'd long gotten over her daddy abandonment issues. Finding out now that he'd tossed money at his inconvenience didn't make it better.

"You said earlier that people are interested in

your daddy lately, meaning I'm not the first person to ask you about him. And I won't be the last. Your daddy was an important man in some circles."

"So what?"

"Meaning some folks think you, as his only child, might be useful to them now that he's dead."

"They'll be sadly disappointed to realize being Theodore Russell's daughter doesn't mean squat."

"It does when they think your daddy left you something."

Did he know about the box, or was he fishing? He might even be friends with those thugs who'd confronted her the other night. "Listen, I don't know what my dead father was involved in, but it has nothing to do with me. So keep me out of it."

"Afraid that might not be possible, honey."

"My name is Dr. Friedman."

"I'm Griffin. But you can call me honey." He had his thumbs hooked in the belt loops of his jeans. A handsome guy. The wrong kind of guy. The type she never got involved with.

"I'm only going to tell you once—move out of my way."

"Not until we figure out this thing with your father."

"What part of 'he's dead' and 'I want nothing to

do with it, him, or you' do you not grasp? Did you hit your head the other night?"

"Head's fine, but you need to give yours a shake. I'm here to help."

"Help me how?" She arched a brow. "By intimidating me?"

"I'm trying to help you avoid another attack. That break-in at your place wasn't an accident."

The knot in her stomach tightened. "How do you know about that? Were you involved?"

"'Course not." A hot denial on his part.

"How am I supposed to believe that when you admitted to spying on me?"

"I wouldn't call it spying. More like keeping an eye on, especially now that I know you're involved."

"You're crazy. I'm not involved in anything. Go away."

"You might be in danger. Your father had enemies."

"He did. Not me." But more than ever, she wondered what the box contained. She should have burned it, given it appeared to be the root of all her recent trouble.

"I can see you're not ready to listen. When you are, come find me at Lanark Leaf."

"Isn't that a pot shop?" She vaguely recalled it as

the name of the one Brandy dragged her to over the weekend.

"I own it. A chain of them, actually. Name's Griffin Lanark. Tell whoever is working to get a hold of me."

"Never going to happen."

"For your sake, I hope you don't have to."

"That sounds like a threat."

"If I wanted you scared, you'd know it." That claim was even more ominous before he melted into the shadows, leaving Maeve staring.

She snapped out of her fugue and rushed to her car, driving home more quickly than the speed limit. She pulled into her garage, her routine of waiting for the door to close familiar, even if more fraught with tension.

Why would she be in danger because of a father she'd never known? According to her mother, he'd left before she'd turned two. She'd never seen a picture, only heard the insults. An asshole for abandoning his daughter. A deadbeat who had no sense of responsibility. A man with no interest in meeting his kid. Surely her mother hadn't lied. It wasn't as if she could ask her. Mom died three years ago in a stupid house fire.

Still, Maeve soon found herself in the basement,

digging around for the box she'd hidden the other day while drunk on a few glasses of wine.

She found it behind the Christmas stuff, a legal-sized cardboard box that she carried upstairs and set on her kitchen table. Opening it sober seemed a monumentally bad idea, so she poured a glass of merlot and leaned against her counter, staring at the box.

What did it contain?

Didn't matter. She should burn it. She wanted nothing to do with the man who'd abandoned her. Only, according to Griffin, Theodore Russell hadn't completely left her adrift. She'd always wondered how her mother had managed to cover her university expenses on a salary that had forced them to pinch pennies and cut as many corners as they could.

She chugged the wine, poured another glass and opened the box. On top sat a folded sheet of lined paper.

Gulp. It took another half a glass of merlot before she could get her trembling hands to open it.

Inside was a handwritten missive.

To Maeve, my daughter.

She put the letter down and chugged more wine. She shouldn't read it. Why bother? It wouldn't do any good. She poured another glass, took a sip, and picked up the letter.

To Maeve, my daughter.

I know you probably hate me and with good reason. This isn't about asking for an apology, although I am sorry I left and we never got to know each other. I wanted to keep you safe and knew of only one way how. By staying away. But if you're reading this, then I'm dead. And you should know I wish I could have had more than the pictures your mother sent me of your progress. Wish I could have told you how proud I was of your grades in school. Of my awe at the woman you've become. In this box is the only legacy I have left. Passed down through many generations of my family. Now passed on to you, where it will finally end. I know this doesn't make sense, and you're probably going to torch the contents of this box. Probably for the best. Some secrets are best left undiscovered. But what I won't hide now are my regret and love for my only child. Be happy, Maeve.

Love, your dad.

Tears tracked down her cheeks. A surprise, given she had no emotional connection to the person who'd written the note. Yet, in a few lines, he'd apologized and made it seem as if he'd had no choice, that abandoning her was the noble thing to do.

Which made her suddenly wonder, had her dad been a criminal? Everything she'd heard and experienced so far pointed to him being some kind of badass. Maybe even a mob boss.

She eyed the box. She should destroy it. Should she look inside first? Did she want to know what it contained?

Those thugs in the parking lot wanted it. Griffin had indicated the break-in was because of her deceased father, which probably meant they wanted the box too. They could have even been the same criminals.

Why now? And why would her father suddenly involve her?

She put the letter aside and glanced inside the box to find a pile of pictures, some she knew all too well, as they were the portraits of her that were taken every year in school, but she also recognized others. Birthday images of her blowing out candles. Her prom. Deeper inside, she came across older, yellowing images that depicted strangers. One of those unfamiliar faces caught her eye—a big man, dark of hair, square of face, appeared in most of them. However, a picture of that man with his arm around a young version of her mother, who held a tiny bundle, sealed it.

Maeve stared at her dad. Finally, she had a face to put to the name.

The next thing she knew, she tore through the

rest of the box, though it didn't contain much beyond the thick pile of photos—a pink blanket sealed in a plastic bag that she'd wager belonged to her, a dog-eared paperback of *The Stand* by Stephen King and, wrapped in bubble wrap several layers thick, a binder. Within that, plastic sleeves held yellowed paper, some of it quite old, the ink faded in spots. She squinted to try to read them, but the words appeared to not be in English or French, the only two languages she really recognized. If she had to guess, her father had left her some old family recipes. He shouldn't have bothered. She didn't cook.

This was what those thugs were after? There was nothing of value here. Just some sentimental junk.

She left the contents scattered on the table and went to bed with the bottle of wine. Door closed. Aluminum bat on the mattress with her.

Ready for trouble.

8

IN CASE OF TROUBLE, Griffin spent the night on the doctor's roof, keeping watch despite knowing she'd freak if she found out he was there.

Too fucking bad. As it turned out, the break-in the other night hadn't been a fluke.

Earlier that day, he'd received a call. Griffin usually ignored calls from unknown numbers, but feeling testy and ready to blast a grifter, he'd answered.

"Okay, asshole, what's the scam today? You coming to arrest me for unpaid taxes? Did I win a trip?"

A huffing and harried voice said, "Is this Griffin Lanark, Alpha of the Byward Pack?"

The mention of his gang by name had him immediately suspicious. "Who's asking?"

"My name is Dwayne Roberts. I am Theo Russell's lawyer."

Russell was Alpha of the Toronto GoldenPaw Pack. "What can I help you with?"

"Theo Russell is dead. His nephew killed him." A blunt statement.

Having already heard the rumors via friends living in Toronto, the information didn't completely surprise Griffin. Apparently, Theo's nephew Antonio had challenged him, and many were accusing the younger man of cheating and killing Theo in an unfair fight.

Apparently, no one had witnessed the battle that took place between uncle and nephew. The Pack had only Antonio's claim that he'd pinned the bigger, wilier wolf—death not required for victory, just a proper latching onto the opponent's neck until he ceded. According to Antonio, a defeated Theo couldn't handle the shame and had thrown himself into Lake Ontario. His body had yet to surface, and more than a few in the GoldenPaw Pack called Antonio a liar and refused to acknowledge him as new Pack leader.

It left the very large and powerful GoldenPaw Pack in a state of turmoil. With them rejecting Antonio's bid for power, who would take over? Would their trouble spill over and affect Griffin's Pack? All good questions that didn't explain why Theo's lawyer was calling.

A door slammed on the other end of the line, and he heard the ding of an elevator. "Why are you calling to tell me this?" Griffin asked.

"Because someone in your Pack is poking at Maeve Friedman."

The mention of her name raised his brows. "What's she got to do with anything?"

"She's Theo Russell's daughter."

He uttered a low whistle. "Well, damn. Would have never known, though I'm not sure why that's a problem."

"Because, despite all the precautions we took, Antonio found out about her."

"Still don't see the issue. She's female. She can't inherit the Pack, or is this because Russell didn't leave the nephew anything in his will?"

"More like she got something she wasn't supposed to, and Antonio will stop at nothing to get it." Footsteps echoed on concrete.

"Are you underground?" he asked.

"Parking lot. Leaving town before his thugs come back to finish the job."

"Are you saying Antonio attacked you?"

"Not directly. The pissant is too much of a coward, which is why no one believes him about Theo.

He plays dirty. Doesn't follow the old ways." Meaning he didn't fight with fang and claw but modern weapons.

"Will he hurt Maeve?"

"I think he'll hurt anyone who gets in his way since he didn't get the GoldenPaws to roll over."

"You think he's in Ottawa?"

"Yes. I've got it from a close source. His girlfriend is pissed at him and claims he's determined to shove his way into an Alpha spot elsewhere."

"And he thought he'd have better luck here?" Griffin snorted.

"Rumor is you were shot the other day. Consider this a tip as to who might have done it. But that's not the real reason I'm calling. I went against Theo's wishes when he died. I involved his daughter."

Beep-beep. The sound of a car unlocking and then a chiming indicated the lawyer was in his vehicle.

"How much does she know about her father? Us? Have you warned her she might be in danger?"

"She knows nothing. Which is dangerous, given I added something to the box I sent to her. I just couldn't destroy it like Theo wanted."

"Destroy what?"

Before the lawyer could answer, a nasally voice in

the background said, "Thanks for confirming she has it, old man."

Griffin heard a popping noise, then another, followed by a thud. The open line remained silent until another voice screamed, "Someone call an ambulance. He's been shot!"

Griffin had hung up, taken everything he'd just learned and tossed it at Dorian, his hacker. He'd roped in Wendell as well to check out the financial implications for both the GoldenPaws Pack and Maeve.

Within a few hours, they'd confirmed the lawyer's story, or at least the parts they could.

Theo Russell had died, and his nephew had taken credit, but the Pack rejected his claim. The guy refused to go away quietly. Their ally in the other Pack told of threats being made and people being intimidated. Not only was the lawyer who'd called Griffin found dead but his secretary was too.

What no one in the GoldenPaw Pack seemed to know? Theo Russell had a daughter. According to Wendell, daddy Russell had supported her financially as a child and student but had kept it a secret. So secret that when the authorities did finally declare Theo Russell dead, the money for his estate would enter a trust fund for the GoldenPaw Pack. His daughter was not mentioned in his will. Yet

Dwayne, the lawyer, had implied he'd sent her something. Something that now put her in danger.

Given Maeve wasn't Pack, that usually wouldn't be Griffin's problem. However, Billy, with his police connections, had advised them that the guy who'd jumped out of his trunk had been identified. He'd belonged to the GoldenPaw Pack and was known to be part of Antonio's close circle. That changed everything.

Griffin's city was under attack. His Pack was being threatened. And what was he doing? Babysitting a woman who wanted nothing to do with him.

He would have called himself all kinds of crazy if a car hadn't pulled to the curb, spilling trouble onto the sidewalk.

9

MAEVE WOKE, and it took a moment for her to realize why. Her home hub, perched on her nightstand, swirled with color, on silent mode for the night but still tracking motion outside. She sat up and snagged her phone, connecting to the online video being captured by her doorbell camera.

Despite the grainy nighttime recording, she could see four people in front of her place. One tall person seemed to be confronting three others.

Turning on the audio, she tried to listen to what they were saying, but she couldn't understand any words—until the tenor of the dispute rose.

"Should have died, motherfucker." One of the men on the sidewalk suddenly lifted a gun.

She put a hand over her mouth, gasping as the big guy moved, his foot arcing to kick the weapon from the other fellow's hand. He kept spinning but also dipping, hooking the legs of another guy and dumping him on his ass. The third dove to attack, only to have his fist blocked, leaving him open to a blow to the jaw.

The first two advanced again as the third recovered. The fellow confronting them didn't retreat. He moved in a blur, fists flying, feet dancing, his movements fluid, graceful, effective.

One man against three. A man she knew. And when it was finished, he remained the last one standing, arms crossed over his chest.

He loudly growled, "Get the fuck out of my town, because if I see you again, you're dead."

The beaten thugs climbed into a car and sped off, leaving behind the tall man, who glanced back at her home as if looking right into the camera.

As if Griffin knew she watched.

"Go back to bed, honey," he said. "I'll keep you safe."

The smart thing would have been to call the cops. Never mind the fact that he might have prevented another break-in, he still seemed to be stalking her.

While she tucked the phone in her robe pocket, she didn't dial. Maeve liked to fight her own battles, and she didn't fear Griffin. Probably a dumb move on her part, given his savage grace and fearlessness when faced with three armed men, yet a certainty existed within that he wouldn't harm her.

Adrenalized, Maeve marched downstairs and flung open the door to find the walkway empty. Where had he gone?

She stepped outside, looking left and right, muttering, "Creepy."

As she whirled to go back inside, a low voice drawled, "Looking for me?"

She almost fell over as she whipped around to face Griffin. "You!" She jabbed a finger in his direction. "You shouldn't be here."

"Shouldn't you be saying thank you for dissuading your nighttime visitors?"

"How do I know they were here to bother me? What if they were following you?"

"No one knew I was here."

"Why are you here? I told you I want nothing to do with you."

"And I told you I'm going to keep you safe. You're welcome, by the way."

She marched up to him and had to angle her head back to match his gaze. "This isn't funny," she hissed. "Find somewhere else to play your macho games. I'm a doctor. I need my sleep."

"Ain't stopping you, honey. Go back to bed. I'll make sure no one disturbs your rest."

"How am I supposed to sleep, knowing you're skulking outside?" she exclaimed, flinging up her hands.

"I guess thinking of me would be distracting. Would you prefer I join you? I'm an excellent cuddler. Although I should warn you—I run hot."

Her mouth rounded before she managed to sputter, "Pervert!"

"Sorry to disappoint, but I ain't into the kinky shit. I like my loving the old-fashioned way. But before you think I'm selfish in bed, I should add I'm all about the giving."

That shouldn't have given her a warm spurt. She lifted her chin. "Not interested. Now go away before I call the cops and report you."

"Report me for what? Having a lovely walk, which you happened to interrupt?"

"Ha! I can prove you're lying. I have video footage of what just happened."

"Do you?" he mocked.

"You're impossible to deal with." She turned to walk away, only to have him slide in front of her.

"I don't mean to frustrate you."

"Are you sure? Because you're doing an excellent job," Maeve grumbled.

"It won't be for much longer. You've been inadvertently caught up in something you shouldn't have."

"Because of you?"

"Because of your father."

A reply that froze her for only a second. "Ironic, given you appear to know him better than I do."

"I wouldn't say I know him, but we met a few times."

"Mob bosses getting together. How nice." A sarcastic retort.

His lips twitched. "An interesting way of seeing it. And while it's not entirely accurate, it's not completely off base."

"There you go again. Admitting something without saying a damn thing. What are you not telling me?"

"Can't a man have some secrets?" His lips tilted, and she fought against his charm.

"Not if they involve other people."

"Don't all secrets apply to others? It's why they must remain untold."

"Nice justification. Does that lie work with your wife?"

"Is this your way of asking if I'm single? Because I am. Never married. Never even engaged. But rest assured, I am a man of experience." He purred the words as he stepped closer.

She tingled. Totally wrong response. She blamed the lack of sleep and the middle-of-the-night wakeup.

She squashed the feeling by latching onto his words. "So you admit you're a womanizer?"

His smile deepened. "Guilty as charged."

"I won't sleep with you."

His hands bracketed the doorframe, making her even more aware of his size. She wasn't actually trapped, but her breath caught as he said, "Who says we'd sleep?"

"Are you seriously propositioning me for sex?"

"Yes."

Rather than slap him and slam the door in his face, she felt her tingles turn into full-fledged desire. Blame the fact she'd not gotten laid in years. Why did her sudden sexual awakening have to be for him? "You're not my type."

"Thank fuck. I'd rather die than turn into some yuppie guy in a suit."

"I think a man in a suit is very sexy." Although she'd be lying if she denied the appeal of Griffin in his molded jeans, slim-fitting tee, and open jean jacket.

"I look best wearing nothing at all." He winked, and once more, her breath caught.

She shouldn't be flirting with her stalker. She also shouldn't be imagining him naked. Would he go away if she slept with him? Or would that just feed the crazy?

"What do you want from me?" she asked, looking into his face.

He met her gaze and held it as he muttered a low, "I want to hear you scream my name as I'm fucking you."

Butterflies stampeded in her belly. She wanted what he offered.

Wanted.

Him.

She should walk away. After all, she wasn't one for casual sex. Or flings. Almost forty and she'd never thrown caution to the wind.

So explain why she grabbed him by the shirt and pulled him down far enough to mash her mouth against his? A clumsy embrace that clanged teeth. She half expected him to push her away for being so aggressive.

Instead, passion exploded. His mouth, hard against hers, immediately took over, caressing and coaxing her lips to part. Tasting and embracing her, igniting all of her senses.

He wrapped a single arm around her waist and, keeping their lips locked, carried her into the house, kicking the door shut behind him, the resulting thud almost enough to break the arousal trance.

But then his hands cupped her ass as his tongue plundered, and she'd never wanted anything so much in her life. Why not have a fling? One night of sex. It didn't have to mean anything. He'd admitted to being a womanizer. He'd probably leave her alone after.

Her gown parted easily, and then his hands and mouth were on her. His lips tugged and teased her nipples, drawing them into erect peaks that he sucked. His hands kneaded her flesh. And when one slipped between her thighs to rub, her hips arched.

With her back pressed to the wall, he dropped to his knees, positioning one of her legs over his shoulder. He then proceeded to lick her, tongue delving, parting her lips, teasing her and flicking her clit. He lashed and sucked and finger-thrust until she cried out and came, her fingers digging into his shoulders. But he wasn't done. He kept teasing until she felt herself tightening again.

Which was when he stood and unbuckled his belt. Through half-lidded eyes, she watched him and reached for the cock that sprang free.

"Condom?" she asked.

"Right here, honey." He pulled a foil packet from his back pocket, and she took it from him and placed it on his shaft. She stroked him, big, hard, long. She wanted him inside her.

She dragged him close and tilted her lips for a kiss, all the while rubbing him. He groaned into her mouth and grabbed hold of her thigh, hoisting it to lace around his hip. He had the height advantage and, with his strength, easily lifted her. She guided the fat head of his dick where she wanted it and sighed as he pushed.

He filled her. Stretched her. With her legs wrapped around him and his fingers digging into her buttocks, she took all of him. Every hard inch.

She might have never had sex standing up, but she had no trouble following his rhythm. And when her head tilted back as passion overtook her ability to keep rocking, he kept the bouncing going, penetrating her just right. Just deep enough. Hard enough.

She came, hissing, "Yes, yes, yes!" And dug her nails into his flesh.

He grunted and went rigid, his body bowing as he found his own pleasure. The pulsing of his shaft only prolonged her own orgasm.

By the time she unclenched, he'd carried her to the living room and sat on the sofa. He kept her in his lap, cock buried inside her, and resumed kissing her.

Surely she'd had enough?

The next climax proved her wrong.

She fell asleep snuggled against his chest.

When her alarm went off, she found herself in a cocoon of arms and legs.

It had really happened.

She shoved out of the warm nest to a low masculine growl of protest. She ignored it, slapped her alarm and ran for the shower. Scrubbing at the stickiness between her legs, she called herself all kinds of stupid. He'd used a condom, but that wasn't a hundred percent. She'd slept with a stranger who'd admitted to being a whore. She'd have to run a full panel on herself.

The least of her worries. She'd eventually have to leave this bathroom and face—

Griffin entered the shower, a big, naked presence. Any protest she might have had died as he hit his knees and said good morning without words.

She thanked the cold tile wall for holding her upright, since her fingers got no traction on his wet skin as she came on his tongue. Then again on his dick.

When he rumbled, "Pass me the soap," she

handed it over and escaped with a squeaked, "I'm going to be late for work."

She jumped into some clean scrubs and tore down the stairs, twisting her damp hair into a bun. As she hit the kitchen for coffee, she noticed the contents of her father's box strewn over the table. She swept everything back in and then took it to the garage to dump into her trunk. She'd dispose of it all in the recycling bin at work.

Griffin walked into the kitchen as she finished pouring sugar and cream into her travel mug.

"Morning, honey." He appeared quite at ease, wearing only a towel around his hips. It drew her attention to the V. His abs. His—

"What happened to the bullet holes?" She finally got a proper look at his upper body and noticed only red welts where there should have been scabbing holes.

"Told you I'm a quick healer."

"That's more than quick." She neared, ready to touch, only to have him snatch her hand and kiss the palm of it.

"Let me make you a proper breakfast."

"I don't have time. I'm going to be late."

"Call in sick." His hand cupped her butt and tugged her against him. Against his erection.

He wanted her again. For some reason, in the

light of day, it made her blush. She pushed away, muttering, "Gotta go."

"Your loss, honey," were his parting words.

The last thing she saw as she backed into the street was the man who'd rocked her world standing on the porch, still in only that towel, sipping coffee from a mug and wearing a smug grin.

A man she barely knew in her house. Utterly crazy. What did it say about her that she thought about turning around and calling in sick? Apparently, she didn't understand how this one-night-stand thing worked.

10

GRIFFIN'S GRIN faded as Maeve drove off. The urge to follow tightened his gut. She'd be fine—the lie he told himself. The confrontation last night had proved the danger to her well-being. While Griffin had fought off those thugs, that didn't mean they'd heed his warning. Most likely, they'd be back, wanting something from his honey.

Yes, *his*. One taste of her, and suddenly his world had tilted. He was in fucking love. And love for a Lycan wasn't just an emotion but a chemical reaction. There would be no other woman for him. Which meant he'd better keep her safe.

As she turned off the street, he reentered her house and hunted down his clothes. Their passion had literally exploded. One minute arguing, the next she'd kissed him, the taste of her the ambrosia he'd been looking for his entire life.

He had to protect her. That started with a tour of her property, looking for the weak spots in her security. Too many windows, and the upper ones were unsecured, as he well knew. A front door and a sliding one into the yard, plus a garage with access to the kitchen. It would take a few days to get a proper alarm system installed. If she agreed.

One night of excellent sex hadn't completely softened her. She'd melted for him in the shower but then had run off the moment she could. Did she expect him to spend the day in her house? Did she want him gone before she finished work? They'd not talked about anything.

Ugh. Love had already ruined him.

Maybe he should be a little less desperate and let her sleep alone tonight. But then, who would watch over her?

As he exited her house through the garage, which didn't need a code to close, he glanced to this left at the For Sale sign on the property two over. With a bit of work, it would be a decent investment for the area and a great base to keep an eye on Maeve, since he was far from ready for her to move in with him. It was more than just the fact they'd barely met. He'd have a hard time fooling the brilliant, intelligent, observant Maeve. Somehow he'd have to ensure she didn't discover the Lycan secret.

While some Lycans allowed their significant others to know, a good chunk of them preferred to not tell anyone who wasn't Pack, because knowing could cause problems that required less-than-pleasant measures to control. More than one pissed ex had tried to out a boyfriend. A good thing no one listened to addicts—the quickest solution to discredit someone. When needed, more permanent measures were taken.

Thankfully, Griffin had had to deal with that only once since he'd become Alpha of the Byward Pack.

How would Maeve react if she discovered the wolf side of him? He hoped to never find out. Griffin's own dad had never been the same after they'd lost Mom. For six months, they'd tried to save her. Six months of her screaming, "Monster!" every time her husband of seventeen years had entered a room. Six months of her eyeing Griffin with horror, even though he'd not yet been changed. His own mother had been repulsed by his existence. While the cops called her death an accident due to drinking and driving, Griffin knew better. It was his fault. It probably explained why the majority of his relationships were about sex and not much else.

But everything felt different with Maeve. The instant connection with her. The need to see her, be with her. Worse now that they'd had sex.

She'd been gone twenty minutes. Had she made it to work safely? Despite his brisk pace to the shop, he pulled out his phone and called.

She answered, "How did you get this number?"

"Hey, honey. Wanted to ask what you'll want for dinner." He played it casual, not about to admit he'd needed to reassure himself. He heard an intercom call for a doctor in the background. She'd made it to work.

"I don't know what time I'm going to be done."

Not quite a rejection, but a casual shove to the side.

He smiled. He'd known she wouldn't make it easy. "I'll make sure to get something easily reheated, then. Any allergies?"

"What are you doing? Why are you acting as if we're suddenly dating?"

"Aren't we?"

"We had sex. No big deal."

"I disagree. What we shared was more than just two people having good sex." Spoken lightly, and yet, annoyance simmered, as she appeared to be making light of what had happened between them.

"Maybe for you. It was only a one-time thing for me."

Full-on rejection. That wasn't supposed to happen. "We can talk about it tonight."

"No, we can't. There is no us." She hung up before he could reply.

Let her avoid him for the night. It would give her time to miss him while he dealt with the danger to her.

The shop hadn't yet opened, and he entered through the back, heading straight up to his apartment. He had some calls to make, starting with Wendell.

"Warning. I'm putting a call in to the country cousins." What he called the gaggle of men who handled the agricultural part of his operation in Northern Ontario. Not all of them were related by blood, but they did have one thing in common—they could all trace their origins to the first Lycan Lanark, who'd changed them.

"Why do we need those inbred idiots?" grumbled Wendell. The older man had once been involved with one of the country cousins. Wendell and Bernard, who seemed more like an uncle to Griffin because of his age, had a history, as in they'd dated for a while until an ugly breakup because of a pregnancy. Bernard got a waitress at a local bar with child, a betrayal that Wendell never forgave. Happened a while ago, but the tension remained.

"I need them because they're good at tracking people."

"In the country. The city is different," Wendell pointed out. "We can find whoever it is ourselves."

"And will you get rid of them?"

The question silenced Wendell. There was a reason some people could be Alpha and some only beta. An Alpha would do anything, even kill, to protect, whereas many a beta would make excuses and attempt forgiveness, causing more grief than was necessary.

Griffin had a great Pack. Good men who were chosen to be his brothers for a reason. But many of them had been born to a new era in which the fist no longer ruled. It didn't make them soft, but it resulted in a need for outside help when they were faced with a truly violent situation.

"Care to explain why we're talking drastic measures?" Wendell asked.

"Do I really need to explain myself?" he asked harshly before launching into the main points. "Let's see, some fucking twat from another city killed his Alpha, along with his lawyer and secretary. That fucker and his gang are now in our city and have already shot me multiple times once. Tried again last night." He didn't mention the part where he'd foiled their plan to go after Maeve.

"Wait, you ran into them again?"

"Yup. Three of them, one with a gun."

"It's an insult they're using weapons," grumbled Wendell.

"I agree, and we can't allow them to keep playing dirty. They have to be stopped."

"Don't see why we need outside help when we outnumber them."

"For now. A dishonorable twat like Antonio might not be bound to keep his bite under control. What if he goes on a spree to turn more men?" The Lycans usually carefully controlled how many they changed, knowing they had to keep a fine balance between enough to not die out but not too many so that they drew attention.

Wendell sighed. "It's actually a distinct possibility, given he was doing it in Toronto."

"What?"

"I'm trying to get it confirmed, but Theo might have caught him making unauthorized Lycans."

Only Alphas got to choose who became Pack—and that criterion varied depending on who did the picking—and they kept those numbers manageable. In a place like Ottawa, Griffin, just like his predecessor, had chosen a baker's dozen—twelve plus him—

although he'd yet to replace two who'd gone on to moonlit pastures. It was well understood that they couldn't just bite people willy-fucking-nilly. For one, not everyone could handle the Lycan virus. Some literally died from it. Others went insane from the pain of the first shift. And in many cases, nothing happened at all because the bite had no effect.

Lycan could only be made, and not easily, despite what the movies claimed. Only men could be changed. Biting women did nothing. And forget being naturally born. Impregnation always ended in death for the mother and fetus. Those who wanted their line to live on made babies before they were changed, and all got fixed once they became Pack to ensure no accidents.

Except for Griffin. Being called a monster by his own mother, the woman who'd cuddled him, hugged him and claimed he was the best thing to ever happen to her, had changed something in him. He'd refused to have kids before his conversion, because he never wanted them to feel how he did—hated by someone he loved so much. His dad tried to get him to change his mind, holding off on giving him the bite, pushing and pleading. He hadn't given up until Griffin had shown him proof that he'd gotten a vasectomy.

He hoped his inability to father children

wouldn't be an issue with Maeve. He knew so little about her. And she would know even less about him. So he'd better make sure the parts she did discover were the good ones.

"Oh, one last thing before I hang up and call the cousins. We're buying a house," Griffin announced.

"What's wrong with your apartment?"

"Nothing. I'll send you the address of the one I want."

"When are you planning to move?"

"I'm not. But I'll want one of the Pack living in it and keeping an eye on another place two houses over."

"Is this about the doctor you spent the night with?"

"If I say yes, will you shut up and take care of it?"

Wendell paused. "Yes, Alpha."

"Thanks, Wendell. Appreciate it."

"Be careful."

"Where's the fun in that?"

11

ALL DAY LONG, in between patients, Maeve thought about Griffin. Of the crazy way she'd thrown herself at him. The pleasure he'd given her. The phone call. The assumption he'd see her again. The way she'd made it clear that last night had meant nothing. At least it shouldn't have. One-night stands weren't supposed to be a big deal, so why did she regret turning down his offer of dinner?

All for the best. A man like him? Not her type. Okay, maybe he was physically—turned out she really liked his big, muscly body—but the rest of him, the whole pot-shop owner and the implied gang bit? Not her scene.

After work, she'd hoped to hang out with Brandy rather than go home alone, but her best friend was going on a date.

"Which guy?" Maeve asked when Brandy told her they couldn't do a girls' night.

"Cute guy I ran into at the coffee shop. We flirted. Exchanged numbers. We're going to a movie."

"Oh. That's awesome." Maeve tried to be excited, only to realize she'd be going home to nothing but anxiety and a frozen dinner.

She half expected to see Griffin waiting for her in the parking lot, but then again, why would he? She'd told him she'd be working late, but then she'd gotten sent home early due to an unidentified smell in the emergency department. They'd cleared people out while they investigated.

Heading home, she gnawed her lower lip. Maybe she'd been too hasty turning Griffin down. After all, a fling didn't have to be restricted to one night. And if she were to be even more honest, she'd felt safe sleeping in his arms. The safest since the break-in. Perhaps she shouldn't have been so hasty about pushing him away.

She eyed her purse, which held her cell phone, debating if she should call. Instead, she rapidly turned before her street and parallel-parked by the Lanark Leaf pot shop. It took her a few breaths to get the nerve to get out of her car. Then a few more to even head for the store.

What am I doing? Would she come across as

desperate? Then again, he'd been the one to call, wanting to see her. She almost talked herself out of her harebrained idea but found her courage and entered the store. An electronic bell raised the head of the guy behind the counter. He was shaggy-headed, mid-twenties at least, wearing a well-washed T-shirt untucked over jeans.

"Welcome to Lanark Leaf. How can I help you today?" A rote query.

She clasped her hands to steady her nerves as she blurted out, "Um, is Griffin here?"

"Who's asking?"

"Dr. Friedman. I mean, Maeve, er, he told me to ask for him?"

"He ain't in right now. But if you leave your name and number, I'll tell him you came by." The young man eyed her up and down, making her uncomfortable.

"Do you know when he'll be back?" She should have texted first.

"Nope, and it ain't any of your business."

The statement rubbed her wrong. "Are you always this rude?"

"You always this desperate?"

The sharp insult had her sucking in a breath, and her cheeks heated. "I see I made a mistake coming here."

"No shit."

The humiliation burned. To think—no, she'd not been thinking. She'd acted out of desperation, loneliness, and horniness.

Rather than subject herself to more insults, she fled. Before speeding home, she hit the grocery store two blocks over from the pot shop, not just for some bread, cheese, and cold cuts but also for a bottle of wine. She needed comfort food and drink. Only then did she head home. She'd barely parked the car in the garage before she was out of it, one arm hugging the paper bag filled with groceries, while her free hand slapped the close button. For once, she didn't wait before heading inside.

Her hands trembled with anger, and shame, as she uncorked the merlot. What had she been thinking, chasing after Griffin? She must not have been the first, given the way that guy had treated her. She gulped the wine and poured a second glass before unpacking her dinner. She'd make herself a charcuterie board and watch something—

Clunk.

The noise swiveled her head, and she eyed the door to the garage. Had she heard something? Probably paranoia. She'd closed the garage door. *But I didn't watch it go all the way down.* What were the chances someone had slipped in?

She told herself she was being foolish even as she poked her head into the garage and blinked at the sight of the gaping maw. The door hadn't closed. She pushed the button, and the door began to descend, only to halt at the three-quarter mark and go back up. Something was impeding the sensor. She moved around her car to see the full opening and found the culprit. A branch lay across the threshold. How had it gotten there? Maybe it had blown in as she'd parked.

Nerves jangling, she moved toward it and bent to pick it up. She barely caught the motion from the corner of her eye. Before she could fully turn, a hand fisted in her hair.

"Ouch!" she screeched and grabbed at the wrist of the person hurting her.

"Where is it?" The low, menacing query had her gasping.

"Leave me alone."

"Not until you hand it over."

He could only be asking about that darned box. If he wanted it, let him have it. "It's in the trunk." She never had found the time to get rid of it. Or maybe she'd lacked the heart to destroy the only things she had of her father.

"Open it." A shove sent her stumbling into the fender of her car. She didn't keep it locked when it was parked in the garage. The latch released, and the trunk lifted, revealing a knapsack with spare clothes in case she needed them at the hospital and a bag full of medical supplies. And nothing else.

No box.

Her assailant realized it at the same moment she did.

"Where is it?"

"I don't know," she huffed. "It was there this morning."

"Lying cunt!"

She might have taken offense at the slur, but all thought was annihilated by the fist to her face that knocked her out.

12

AFTER A DAY SPENT on the phone and computer trying to locate Antonio and his crew, and only getting frustrated, Griffin gladly hit the shower. According to the schedule that Dorian had managed to scrounge from the hospital network, he had another hour at least before Maeve got off work. Longer if she stayed for a bit of overtime.

He planned to be waiting beside her car in the parking lot before she finished her shift. She might have refused dinner with him, but that didn't mean he'd leave her alone and unprotected. He planned to make sure she got home safely. With Antonio's gang on the loose, he couldn't be too cautious.

With that in mind, he didn't want to be late. He finished dressing and eyed the shop's security monitors as he tucked in his shirt. The door was closing on a customer, a woman with long dark hair that reminded him of Maeve's. Fuck, he had it bad.

Thoughts of her were replaced by annoyance as he noted Lonnie was on his phone.

Again.

Lazy fucker. He'd been told to stay off the thing when he worked. Should have never accepted him when the loner had shown up looking for a Pack a few months ago. Lonnie had begged, spinning some sob story about his last Pack tossing him out because of trouble with a girl. At the time, Griffin had felt sorry for the young man. He'd had a hard life. He'd just wanted a chance. But in the time since he'd accepted him into the Pack, Griffin had come to realize he really didn't like Lonnie. Not only was he the laziest fucker but a few of his boys claimed there was something off about the guy. Might be time to cut Lonnie loose.

Griffin headed downstairs to give Lonnie yet another warning. He entered the shop and stopped dead as he smelled his honey. The distinctive scent of her lifted his head, and he swiveled it to check every corner for her.

"Where is she?" he asked Lonnie, since the store held no one else.

"Who?" Lonnie didn't even rise from his slouch. The disrespect almost cost the guy his front teeth.

"Where is Maeve? Why didn't you call me and tell me she was here?" She'd obviously come to find him, because he highly doubted she'd come in to buy another vape when hers remained almost brand new.

"Don't know what you're talking about."

He narrowed his gaze on Lonnie. "Why are you lying to me? I can smell her. She was here. And recently." He thought of the woman he'd seen leaving only moments ago. He'd just missed her.

The younger man finally looked nervous. "Oh, you mean the chick that just came in? I sent her away."

"You did what?" The words emerged as a low growl.

"Just doing you a favor. Figured she was some floozy—"

His fist hit Lonnie in the jaw before the fucker finished speaking. The young man stumbled back into the wall, hard.

"What did you do that for?" Lonnie whined.

"Watch your fucking mouth when you talk about Maeve."

Lonnie rubbed his jaw and eyed him resentfully. "Didn't know she was your girlfriend."

"Doesn't matter who she is. Someone comes in and asks for me, you fucking call me. You don't tell them to fuck off."

"Well, now I know," Lonnie snarked.

The attitude rubbed him even more wrong. "You mouthy little fucker. I've had it. Get out."

"You can't just fire me."

"I can do whatever I fucking like, you little shit. And I've had enough of you. So consider yourself ex-Pack."

"You're kicking me out?" Lonnie's jaw dropped. "Over some fucking chick?"

"Not just any chick. *My* fucking chick. I swear, if you screwed things up with her..." He could think of only one reason for her to show up here. She wanted to see him.

Good. Because he wanted to see her. But first, he stripped a sulking and bitching Lonnie of his keys, ignored his threats of, "You'll fucking regret this," and locked up the shop. Then he headed into the back to find the office empty, so he texted Dorian to remove all of Lonnie's electronic access, which resulted in a short exchange that required few words to convey a lot.

Griffin: Fired Lonnie.

Dorian: About time.

Griffin: Remove all access.

Dorian: Done.

Griffin: Going to Maeve's.

Dorian: See you tomorrow.

He hoped she wasn't pissed. What the fuck possessed Lonnie to kick her out?

By the time Griffin left, about twenty minutes had passed. He didn't drive over since she lived so close. Hands shoved into his jacket pockets, he stalked to her place, passing by the grocery store before turning up an alley to cut across to where she lived. He almost stopped for food and flowers, but something pushed him to get to her quickly. A man who trusted instinct, he didn't fight the driving imperative.

When he arrived at her house, no lights were on despite the darkening sky. Perhaps she'd not gone straight home after leaving his shop. Her garage had no window, so he couldn't check for her car, but the distinct smell of exhaust lingered in her driveway, as if a vehicle had recently been there. Odd, though, the branch on the tarmac. It must have fallen after she'd parked, given it remained uncrushed.

He knocked firmly on the front door. No answer. A step back allowed him to eye the house. The plywood on the living room window meant he couldn't see inside.

Scuff.

The faintest noise indicated someone moved around inside. The hair on his body lifted as he sensed something amiss.

He highly doubted Maeve was inside and ignoring him. She didn't strike him as the type to ghost him.

He knocked again. "Maeve, honey, you home?" He paused to listen, not just with his ears. There was that creak of the stair. Someone headed upstairs. He pretended to slowly walk away. He paused and glanced at the house. The person watching at the upstairs window jerked hard enough that the curtain rustled.

He had a feeling that hadn't been his honey. He strode away from the house, trying to look casual, having to go farther than he would have liked before doubling back. The house for sale remained easy to enter, and he quickly made his way to the second floor and the window he'd used before.

Nightfall did much to help hide his blatant dash across the rooftops to Maeve's home. The window to her bedroom remained unlatched.

He entered quietly, the scent of her surrounding him. With careful steps, he made his way to the door and then the staircase. Avoided the squeaky step. Tightened in anger as he heard a distinctly male voice sounding threatening. Before making a move, he fired off a quick text to let some of his boys know what was happening. Then he crept closer.

"So much for rescue, doctor lady. Your boyfriend

is gone, and by the time he comes back, we'll be done with our chat."

"I told you I don't know where it is. Someone must have stolen it from my trunk while I was at work or the grocery store."

Hearing her voice did nothing to ease Griffin's anger. On the contrary, it only hardened it. Who dared to threaten her?

"I'm sure you'll remember if we start cutting off body parts. Can't be a doctor with no fingers." A threat punctuated by the slide of a blade as it was pulled from a knife block.

"What's so darned important about that box? It's just a bunch of pictures, most of them old."

"Don't know. Don't care, other than it's worth a grand in cash to whoever brings it to him."

"I can pay you double to leave me alone."

"Make it $10K, or I start cutting."

Griffin had heard enough. He stepped into view, drawing the eye of the burly fellow leaning over Maeve with a butcher knife in his hand.

"Well, well, look who came back. I thought he didn't have a key." The fellow with the strong body odor pinched Maeve's chin hard.

"He doesn't," she mumbled. "I don't know how he got in."

"Why don't you pick on someone more your size,

coward?" Griffin taunted, fully entering the kitchen and angling sideways, forcing the man to shift to keep him in sight. He didn't recognize this guy with the shaved head. The fucker was big and tall, tattooed and mean-looking. But not wolf.

"Surprised you're out of the hospital already. Could have sworn I shot you in the heart." The idiot —who hopefully did not procreate—admitted to being one of the gunmen.

"Guess your aim is shit," Griffin stated, doing his best to not stare at Maeve after allowing himself only a quick glimpse. Anger bubbled beneath the surface at her swollen lower lip and the bruise already forming on her cheek. The thug had her tied to a chair.

"That's because guns ain't my thing. But knives, though... Always did prefer carving." The guy grabbed Maeve by the hair and yanked her head back, placing the blade against her flesh.

To her credit, she didn't whimper, but her scent sharpened with fear.

It took everything in Griffin to not act. The slightest wrong word or flex of a limb and she might find her throat slit. He needed to distract the guy. Separate him from his honey.

"Who hired you?" Griffin asked.

"Doesn't matter."

"I'm surprised you're still employed, given how you failed to kill me."

The thug didn't like the insult and pricked Maeve's flesh hard enough that a bead of blood formed. "Then guess this time I'll have to make triple sure you're dead. Maybe I'll bring the boss your head."

"Kill me, and you won't ever find the package." A wild guess as to why the dead man walking had gone after Maeve.

His claim snagged the guy's attention. "Where is it?"

"I am not telling you a fucking thing until you move away from Maeve."

"Tell me where it is!" The thug lifted the knife from her flesh and waved it in Griffin's direction. Not ideal.

Before Griffin could act, Maeve did!

Her upper body might have been restrained, but her legs remained loose, and she scissored them, tangling them around the knife wielder's. The motion was rapid and startling enough that she threw the guy off-balance. Not one to waste an advantage, Griffin rushed in. A few powerful fists to the fucker's head and his eyes rolled back. He would have liked to hit him more, but Maeve was watching.

He dropped the limp body to the floor and

turned to Maeve. She did her best to try to wriggle out of the tape binding her upper body.

"Hold still while I cut you loose." Griffin plucked the knife from the floor and used it to carefully saw through the sticky pieces.

"How did you get in?" she asked, rather than thank him for coming to her rescue.

He paused his cutting to eye her. "Is that part important?"

"It is, considering you had no way of knowing I was in danger and I didn't hear the front door getting kicked in."

"Let's just say I acted on a gut feeling." He finished slicing through the tape and took a step back as she flexed her arms to loosen it before peeling it away.

"Do your gut feelings often lead you to breaking and entering?" was her tart reply.

"A good thing it did this time, wouldn't you say?" Then, because he knew she lashed out only because she'd been scared, he shifted her focus. "I heard you came looking for me at the shop."

"I did and was succinctly told you weren't interested."

"Lonnie is a fucking liar. I fired his ass."

She paused in peeling off the tape. "You fired him for telling me to go away?"

"Yes."

Her lips curved but only for a half-second before she frowned again. "So you came to explain and apologize? Still doesn't explain how you got in."

"Bedroom window. I remembered seeing it unlocked." A reminder of the night they'd spent together.

It didn't distract her sharp mind. "There's no way to climb up to my window. That's the only reason I don't latch it," she pointed out, shoving the tape she'd removed in the garbage can. She then eyed the roll on the counter and the guy drooling on her floor.

Before she could even think of it, Griffin snared the roll and hit his knees, binding the man's wrists so if he woke, he could do no harm.

"Well?" she asked, tapping her foot.

"I got to your window from the roof."

"The roof. Like a cat burglar." A flat statement.

"How about like the hero who saved your fucking ass?" he snapped, rising to tower over her.

She lifted her chin and didn't cower one bit. "My ass would have been fine if you'd not stolen my box! I would have handed it over, and he"—she glared at the man on the floor—"would have left."

"I don't have the box."

Her mouth rounded. "But you said—"

"I lied to get him to change his focus from you to me."

Her lips pursed. "If I don't have it, and you don't have it, then who does?"

"I don't know. But given how badly someone wants it, we should find out."

13

WE.

Maeve wasn't sure how she felt about his use of that word. He talked as if they were a team. A couple. As if she'd get involved with someone who thought nothing of climbing onto a roof to break into her house.

What about the fact he'd saved her from harm? Did that negate his actions?

A part of her wanted to say yes. Blame the epic sex. That part of her wanted to see the good in him to justify her desire.

On the other hand, she couldn't help but feel the trouble she'd encountered occurred partially because of him, which wasn't really fair. In reality, she'd been assaulted because of her dad.

Why did someone want the box so badly? Since

she doubted the pictures or paperback were to blame, she had to wonder just what the binder contained. Apparently, something that justified torturing a woman to get it.

She eyed the man on the floor and had to restrain an urge to kick him. It would have been well deserved, given the throbbing in her cheekbone. She'd have a shiner, for sure. Would have to explain the assault at work because if she didn't, then she had no doubt she'd receive not-so-subtle pamphlets on her desk about domestic abuse. She'd gotten a whole stack of them after she'd given herself a shiner with a rake. No one believed she'd actually stepped on one and smacked herself in the face. She'd had the dumb grass replaced with stone after that.

"We should call the police," she abruptly announced. A police report might help with the hospital gossip.

Griffin opened his mouth, and she readied herself to argue when he refused. Instead, he said, "Already called."

"You did?" Color her surprised.

"Yup. Sent out an SOS for help the moment I knew you were being held hostage. Contrary to your apparent belief, I am a law-abiding kind of guy."

"You don't fight like one." He'd shown no reticence about pummeling her assailant.

"I grew up in a rough area. Had to know how to defend myself. And you're one to talk. The way you tripped him up? That was brave."

She grimaced. "Not really. I was terrified and didn't know what else to do." In her mind, she'd hoped to trip her attacker so that he'd fall on the knife. Although Griffin handling him proved a better, less-bloody solution for her kitchen floor.

"Where else did he hit you?" he asked, reaching out to gently cup the uninjured side of her face.

"Just a punch to the cheek, hard enough to knock me out." She grimaced.

"How do you feel?"

"Sore," she admitted. "But seemingly fine otherwise. No ringing in the ears or blurred vision. Too soon to say if I have a concussion, though."

"I'm sorry."

"Why? Admitting this is your fault?"

"In a sense. If Lonnie hadn't fucking sent you away, then you and I would already be in my apartment and this wouldn't have happened."

"Or it would have delayed it, and instead of you arriving in time, I'd be missing a few fingers." Her stomach roiled as she said it. She'd meant to sound light, only to be hit by the harsh reality. That man would have hurt her more than he already had.

She suddenly ran for the nearest bathroom so she

could hit the floor in front of the toilet. She, a woman who could stick her hands inside another person's flesh to fix wounds, puked at the thought of what almost happened.

The gagging went on until her empty stomach stopped convulsing. She hugged the porcelain, eyes closed against the burning tears of shame and latent fear.

A hand gently laid against her back stiffened her. "You okay, honey?"

The soft query had her blinking at him, surprised, because she'd never had someone by her side while she was puking. Most people stayed away.

"I'll live," she croaked.

He rubbed her back lightly. "I brought you some water to rinse out your mouth."

"Thanks." She reached for the proffered glass and took a big drink to swirl in her mouth. He rose and left before she spat in the toilet. She did it again and flushed before rising. Her blotchy reflection in the mirror had her grimacing.

Griffin returned, this time holding a damp cloth. Warm, she noticed when she wiped it across her mouth and chin.

"Sorry," she mumbled, unable to meet his gaze in the mirror.

"For what? Being human? I'm surprised it took that long for the shock to hit you."

"He told me he'd cut off my fingers." She tasted a sourness in her mouth as she said it aloud.

"I'm sorry, honey. I wish you'd never had to go through that." He drew her to his chest, a big chest, and wrapped his strong arms around her, making her feel safe.

She didn't know how long they stood there, hugging in her tight main-floor bathroom. She was okay with them standing there forever, but she didn't argue when he led her by the hand upstairs, saying, "You should brush your teeth. You'll feel better."

The doorbell rang just as she went up the first step. She paused.

"Go. Freshen up." He waved her on. "I'll let the cops in and fill them in on what happened."

She wanted to argue, but she also wanted to remove the acrid taste from her mouth. She wouldn't be long. She ran upstairs and into her bathroom, only to cringe at the sight of her face. Not just blotchy from puking but swollen where the thug punched her. She'd grab an ice pack when she went back down. She scrubbed her teeth and tongue. Washed her face thoroughly and then applied some witch hazel to the throbbing parts of her face. It should ease some of the swelling.

She took a second to brush her hair and take a deep breath. More than likely, the police would want her to go to the station for a statement. She should pack snacks. She might not be hungry now, but eventually it would hit her, since she'd yet to have dinner.

As she went down the stairs, she heard the murmur of voices. She walked into her kitchen to find the body on the floor gone and Griffin chatting with Detective Gruff.

Both immediately greeted her, Griffin moving to her side, the detective offering a nod. "Your friend was just telling me about your home invasion."

She didn't evade the comforting arm Griffin placed around her. Being a strong woman at work and in life didn't negate the fact that it was sometimes nice to have someone to lean on.

"He came in through the garage." It irked Maeve that it happened the one time she hadn't been watching to prevent that exact scenario. "Where is he?" she asked, even as she silently prayed no one answered that he'd escaped.

"Taken to the station for processing," Detective Gruff stated.

"I guess I need to go make a statement." Dread filled her. This would suck.

"Actually, Mr. Lanark has already told us more

than enough details to charge the perpetrator. No need for you to do anything at this time."

She couldn't deny the relief at knowing she wouldn't spend hours at the precinct. "If you need more information, then let me know. I don't want to see that guy walking free anytime soon."

"He won't hurt you again," Griffin softly vowed. The detective didn't bat an eye at the implied threat. "Can you tell me more about the box the perpetrator was looking for?"

She shrugged. "Not much to say other than I assume it's the one I received from my father. He died, and a lawyer sent some of his stuff. Mostly pictures of him, a book, and a binder."

"What was in the binder?" Griffin was the one to ask.

"Don't know. I couldn't read the writing. Looked old. If I were to guess, recipes of some kind. They seemed to have ingredient lists, followed by instructions. Oh, and a few doodles of plant leaves."

"Sounds like a possible family heirloom," Griffin mused aloud.

"No idea because I never knew my father's side."

"The box is missing?" the detective clarified.

She nodded. "I put it in my trunk this morning, and it was gone by the time my attacker showed up. And good riddance. It's been nothing but trouble."

"I hate to even mention this," the detective said slowly, "but there is a strong possibility, given your recent issues, that the guy sitting in jail might not be the only one to come after that box."

"But it's gone."

"They won't necessarily know that."

"Meaning what? That I'm still in danger?"

"Yes." The detective didn't sugarcoat it. "Is there somewhere else you can stay for the next little while?"

"I guess I can go to a hotel." Anywhere but here. Her haven no longer felt safe.

"Like fuck you are," Griffin growled. "She'll be staying with me."

She turned on him, mouth rounded. "I can't do that."

"Why not? I've got the space."

"Because we barely know each other."

"I know you snore in your sleep," he pointed out, despite the fact they had an audience.

"Do not."

"It's okay. I think it's cute." He winked.

The detective cleared his throat. "Staying with someone is probably a better idea than being on your own."

"I can go to Brandy's." Her small apartment would be tight, but it would be only temporary.

"So you'd rather put her in danger?" Griffin drawled.

Her cheeks heated with annoyance. "No."

"Then it's settled. Pack a bag, honey."

"What if I don't want to stay with you?" she huffed.

"You really want to be stubborn about this?"

"Um, I'll let you two hash this out. Ma'am, I'll be in touch if we need anything." The detective walked out, leaving her facing off against Griffin.

She pinched her lips together. "Just because we slept together doesn't give you the right to order me around."

"It's not an order, it's an invitation. Come on, honey, we both know you'll be safest with me."

"Safe with a drug dealer. Sounds like an oxymoron."

"You forgot the part where I'm a hundred percent legit in the eyes of the law with an apartment protected by an alarm system and other security." He grabbed her hands when he added, "I know this isn't your first choice, but it's only temporary."

"Once whoever wants my father's damned box realizes I don't have it, they'll stop coming after me." Stating it aloud didn't convince her.

What did? Griffin saying, "Anyone comes after you, and they'll have to go through me first."

14

RATHER THAN GO in through the back of the shop, where he might run into some of his curious Pack, Griffin took Maeve through the front, locking the door right away and disarming the alarm then rearming it.

Maeve said nothing, just waited with her bag slung over her shoulder. She wouldn't let him carry it, but she had let him drive her car after he'd pointed out her shaking hands.

"I live on the second and third floors." He let her go up first and, being a man, enjoyed the sight of her ass every time the fabric of her slacks tightened over it with each step.

At the top, she waited while he entered the code to unlock the door. There was also a key, in case the power went out, well hidden, its whereabouts known only by him.

They entered, and she uttered a soft, "Wow."

"You like?" For some reason, her response mattered. He'd been rather proud of what he'd achieved. Reclaimed pinewood floors. The walls freshly plastered. New windows that were larger and more energy efficient.

"It's nice. I like how open it is." She slipped off her shoes before wandering to explore. Her first stop had her running her hand over the granite slab of his kitchen island. She set her bag on its surface.

"This is the main living area, obviously. Upstairs is the bedroom and bathroom."

"You must have a lot of friends," she observed, gazing in the direction of his couches and club chairs.

"A few. Most work for me, and this is where we conduct company meetings most of the time."

"I'm obviously in the wrong profession," she muttered, eyeing the massive television on his wall.

"You have a much more important job than me. Not to mention expensive classes to take."

Her nose scrunched as she said, "Took me almost ten years to pay off the loans. Now I'm working on my mortgage."

"If it makes you feel better, I'm still paying for the renovations."

She suddenly grinned. "Actually, that does make me feel better."

Her smile warmed him from head to toe. "You hungry?" he asked.

The query turned her lips down. "No. I can't stop thinking about what happened." She palmed her stomach as if she felt queasy again.

"You're safe. The fucker's in jail." He wasn't, actually. When Griffin had sent the SOS to Billy, it had been to avoid other cops showing up. Her puking and then going upstairs had given Billy the opportunity to get the thug out of there.

"That thug who attacked me... He said someone hired him, meaning this isn't over. I wish there was a way to let whoever it is doing this know I don't have the box anymore." She rubbed a hand over her face. "Who knew the man who couldn't be bothered to be a father while alive would make my life difficult while dead?"

"I'm sure he never intended to."

"Guess we'll never know." A defeated reply.

"I know what will help you relax. I have a jacuzzi tub, with enough jets to turn your body into soft putty."

"Already trying to get me naked?"

He shook his head. "Not tonight." Much as he

wanted to drag her into his arms and make her forget, he wouldn't take advantage of her fragile mental state. She'd suffered a shock. The last thing she needed was him slobbering all over her and mauling her, even if she would orgasm from it. "Why don't you go for a nice soak? Alone."

"And where will you be?"

"Just downstairs. I got some work stuff to handle."

A wary look entered her eyes. "Who has access to your apartment?"

"No one but me. And ain't no one getting past me to those stairs."

"You didn't need stairs or a door to get inside my house."

"This building is too far from its neighbors for anyone to use the same method I did at your place. I promise you're safe. Would you rather I stayed with you?"

She chewed her lower lip before shaking her head. "I'll be fine. I'm just a little more shook than I thought."

"The bathtub is big enough for two," he teased.

The pink in her cheeks almost had him chuckling as she sputtered, "I'm good. You go do what you have to."

"First, let me show you where to find towels and stuff."

She admired his massive bedroom and oohed over his even bigger tub. He left her with his robe hanging on a bathroom hook, a pile of towels for body and hair, and a reminder he wouldn't be far.

As he headed downstairs, he tried to not think of her getting naked and into his tub. What he wouldn't give to join her. But she needed time to settle her head. And pushing her would have the opposite effect.

Besides, Griffin wanted to have a chat with someone.

He found Billy in the basement, along with their prisoner and Ulric, who sat with booted feet on a table.

"Hey, boss man."

"What have you gleaned thus far?" Griffin asked as he peeled off his shirt. Didn't want to get blood on it. Maeve might notice.

"Nothing. The fucker's been tight-lipped."

"Has he? Good, because I'm in the mood to hit something." Griffin allowed a small smile to pull his lips and made sure the thug saw it.

"Go ahead and hit me. I ain't saying shit." The man spat on the floor.

"That's your prerogative." Griffin's jeans and

boxers went next, after he kicked off his shoes and socks.

"Fucking perv. You going to fuck me into submission?"

Griffin rolled his shoulders, flexing and cracking his limbs before he said, "I'm going to show you why you messed with the wrong man."

"Wasn't messing with you. That bitch doctor is the one with something we want."

"And she's under my protection."

"You did a piss-poor job, then," taunted the idiot in the chair.

"I did, which is why I now need to make it right." He glanced at Ulric. "Throw his ass in the room. Time he started talking."

"You got it, boss." Ulric cut the tape binding the man before hauling him to a door, metal and framed into the concrete. A safe room for those who couldn't properly control themselves during the full-moon shifts.

Soundproof. Escape-proof. The twenty-by-twenty chamber held nothing inside. Griffin walked in to find the captive waiting for him in a fight stance.

"Let's go then, perv." The man balled his fists.

The door slammed shut behind Griffin.

He smiled. "This ends when you start talking."

"Gonna take more than you for that."

"Really?" Griffin smiled as he called forth the wolf inside, letting the excruciating pain rip through him as his body reshaped, the virus triggered by pure will in his case. Other Lycans could shift only under the moon.

But an Alpha... An Alpha commanded the wolf.

When he snarled, showing the captive his teeth, it was almost enough for the man to start talking.

Luckily, it wasn't that easy. The idiot thought he could fight, and Griffin got to vent some of his frustration.

By the time Griffin gave the patterned raps on the door, he knew everything and nothing.

He knew the man's name was Travis McDonald and he'd been recently paroled, which happened to be how Antonio had found him. Apparently, the fucker from Toronto spent part of his time outside the parole board office making offers.

Ten grand to kill Griffin.

A grand if the box was retrieved.

As to where Antonio was hiding?

Travis had sworn—and blubbered—he didn't know. He'd been given a number to text for instructions if he were successful.

No need to relay that information, given the camera in the room recorded it all. As Griffin exited,

Ulric handed him a damp towel to wipe away the blood streaking his face.

"Can't believe Antonio tried to turn that piece of shift," Ulric said with disgust.

Tried, according to the bite marks on Travis's arm, but luckily it had failed. A mean man made a mean wolf. Not conducive for a species trying to lie low.

"What do you want us to do with him?" Ulric asked. Billy had left during the interrogation, citing a lead.

"I'm thinking we should do our civic duty and make sure that piece of shit never bothers anyone again."

"Yes, sir." Ulric didn't question the order. Like Griffin and many others in the Pack, he had no patience or tolerance for assholes like Travis. Getting rid of him permanently would make the world a better place.

Before Griffin returned to Maeve, he fetched some Indian takeout from down the street.

He found her perched on a stool in his kitchen, wearing his robe, her hair damp and hanging down her back.

She whirled as he entered, her hand clutching a knife, ready to defend herself. He almost told her the truth, that Travis would never hurt her or anyone else ever again.

Instead, he held up the paper bag of food and shook it. "Don't kill me. I come bearing food."

He would have given her the world when she smiled and said, "My hero."

15

Even after a most excellent dinner, Griffin made no move on Maeve. She kept expecting that. Partly why she'd put on his robe instead of the clothes she'd brought. She'd had time while she'd luxuriated to decide she needed to be less uptight.

Yes, Griffin dealt in marijuana, but as a doctor, she was well aware that not only was it legal in Canada but it also had medical benefits. Would she really judge him on being successful at selling it?

While his method might have been sketchy, the man did come to her rescue. But his heroism hadn't ended there. He'd offered her the use of his place, promised to protect her, brought her food, given her space, and respected her boundaries. In other words, he'd given her everything she needed.

A greedy Maeve wanted more.

Having him sitting by her side made her all too aware of him as a man. Reminded her of the pleasure to be had from his touch. To her annoyance, he insisted on being a damned gentleman.

Which left her with only one real choice.

Boldness.

"Are you ever going to kiss me?"

He paused in midsentence while telling a story involving the renovation to stare at her. "You're probably tired."

"I am. We should go to bed." And then, in case it wasn't clear, she added, "Together."

"Are you sure?" he asked, even as he shifted to draw her onto his lap.

"Never been more certain of anything," she whispered against his lips.

They didn't make it to the bed. Their kiss went on forever, and she found herself lying on the couch, his heavier body atop hers.

Her legs hugged him as he ground against her, just kissing, so much kissing she was breathless and wet. Her entire body clamored for more.

As if sensing her growing need, he slid his lips from her mouth, moving along her jaw, then down the column of her throat. He paused over her pulse, ran his tongue over it, and her breathing hitched.

His hand tugged at the robe, parting the folds, and he half lifted himself to better look at her and play. He stroked his hand down the valley between her breasts to her belly before cupping her.

Her hips twitched, and she would have sworn his eyes flashed for a second. He dove down so that his mouth might follow the path his hand took. He paused to rub his partially grizzled jaw against the soft skin of her belly. His breath teased her as he then slipped those lips over her abdomen and lower. When he blew hotly against the core of her, she trembled.

"You smell so fucking good," he murmured, the words hot exhalations against her sensitive flesh.

She shivered and let her leg fall from the couch, opening herself to him. He growled in appreciation as he pressed against her, giving her an intimate kiss.

"Oh." She managed only that as the wet tip of his tongue traced the lips of her sex, teasing between, flicking her clitoris.

He tongued her, probing and thrusting, until Maeve clutched at the couch cushion, hips straining to get closer to the pleasure. He licked her and circled his tongue around her clit, teasing her until she grabbed his hair.

He chuckled against her flesh, teasing her some more before he resumed his oral torture. On the edge, she bucked, and yet, he stuck close. Licking. Teasing. But pulling back when she was about to come.

She whimpered as her need became too much.

"Look at me, honey." A soft demand.

She opened her eyes and was caught in his gaze.

"Undress me."

While she wore a simple robe that slid from her shoulders as she sat up, he remained fully dressed. She grabbed hold of his plaid shirt, eyed its buttons then him. Grinned.

"I love this shirt," he said.

"I'll buy you another." She yanked, and buttons snapped, making her laugh.

He laughed with her before catching her in another kiss. But she wasn't done. She shoved at him and stroked her hand down his lightly furred chest until she reached the waistband of his pants.

She pushed him. "Stand up."

"Yes, ma'am." He stood, and she reached for the buttons on his jeans, unlooping them one by one, noticing how he tensed and his breathing grew ragged.

She tugged them down and got a face full of cock, those briefs of his unable to contain his erection. When it poked her in the cheek, he exclaimed, "Um, sorry about that."

"Why apologize?" She grabbed hold of him and gave him a coy smile before she sucked the tip.

He gasped.

She sucked him again, making sure he felt the swirl of her tongue.

He groaned.

She would have done more, but he sounded pained as he said, "If you don't stop, I'm going to be useless in, like, thirty seconds."

She paused and glanced at him. Given the fire between her legs, she would hate to waste this opportunity.

"Condom?" she asked.

He almost tripped getting out of his jeans and digging through a pocket. Kind of heady to have a man this virile so attracted to her. She dragged him close for a kiss and stroked his covered erection.

He hissed. "Too close."

"Sit down." She shoved him onto the couch, and he went, his cock jutting up, long and thick. She straddled his thighs, trapping his erection between them. It throbbed as they kissed, their tongues mingling in a sensual duel.

Her nipples pebbled, and he must have felt them, because he cupped her head and leaned her back that he might bend to take one into his mouth. A moan escaped her as his tongue swirled around the nub. She angled her hips into him, looking to put pressure where she needed it most.

She lifted herself enough to grab his cock and rub it against her cleft. Already wet, she honeyed him up before guiding him into her. His fingers dug into her ass cheeks, and he tensed as she pushed down on him. When he'd gone deep, she tilted her hips and ground him even deeper.

He trembled. "Fuck me, honey." His fingers clutched her tight.

"I'm trying," she teased, leaning in to kiss him as she rotated her hips.

She caught his moan and his uneven breaths as she rocked and rolled on his cock. He filled her perfectly, thick enough to stretch, long enough to find her sweet spot. She squeezed around him as she rode, rocking and grinding. Whimpering at the pleasure of it. Losing her rhythm because of it.

He rolled her onto her back, somehow staying buried to the hilt. He held on to her hips as he took over the rhythm, thrusting into her, hitting that sweet spot each time. He pistoned faster and faster, clenching her tighter and tighter.

She barely breathed, and she tensed, her nails digging into his shoulders as pleasure coiled.

When her orgasm hit, she cried out, "Griffin."

She'd have sworn he howled in reply.

Together, they came, with him first shouting and then sucking on her skin, even nipping it as he shuddered against her.

"Mine," he growled, the word possessive, and yet, she luxuriated in it. Craved it. Held tight to him when he carried her upstairs to bed and pleasured her again.

She dug her nails into him as he rode her hard, fast. Her shuddering body tightened as he kept pounding against her sweet spot. Bringing her right back to the edge of that cliff.

She couldn't help but scream as she came again, harder than she'd ever come before. He joined her, groaning her name, buried to the hilt, climaxing inside her and then holding her tight.

There wasn't much to say, even if she could have caught her breath to speak. Instead, she clung to him, her cheek resting against his chest when he rolled to his back, her hand against his heart, which took its sweet time slowing down.

Comforted and satiated, she fell asleep, and only because of the insistent alarm on her phone going off, she woke in time for her shift at the hospital.

"Ugh. Work." She grimaced against his chest.

"Call in sick," he suggested, rubbing his face against the top of her head.

"I can't," she sighed. "We're already short doctors as it is."

"Then I guess we wait for tonight."

"We have time for a quickie." She rotated against him, and he groaned but needed no further invitation. He rolled her to slide into her from behind, his finger working her clit as he thrust, bringing her quickly to orgasm.

She panted in his arms afterward and whispered, "That's better than any breakfast."

"Only because you haven't had my pancakes." He nipped her shoulder. "Go shower while I get your breakfast ready."

"You don't have to," she hastened to reply. "I usually only have a coffee."

"Not today. Go." All thought of arguing fled as he rolled out of the bed and stalked across her field of vision, his tight, naked ass a thing to behold.

If he insisted... She would enjoy it, then. It wasn't often anyone pampered her. Actually, other than Brandy, no one ever did anything for Maeve. She had no living family. Her work didn't allow for an active social life, so she had few friends.

There was something to be said for walking into a kitchen and finding a glass of orange juice beside a full mug of coffee. The moment she sat, Griffin, wearing only boxers, slid a plate in front of her with the fluffiest pancakes and a side of bacon. The man even had real maple syrup.

She groaned at the first bite and murmured, "I think I love you." Only to freeze.

So did he, but only for a second before the corners of his eyes crinkled. "I will relay your compliment to the chef." He turned her awkward gaffe into the lighthearted statement it was meant to be.

But it stuck with her, mostly because she just might well be falling in love.

When he insisted on driving her to work, she protested. "You don't need to do that. It's not far, and the hospital is usually very safe, especially during the day."

She thought he'd argue, but he nodded. "Sorry. I don't mean to be overprotective."

Since she actually liked that he cared, she offered a compromise. "I'll text you the moment I get there."

"You'd better." He dropped a light kiss on her lips and saw her to her car, which he'd parked in the alley between the buildings.

She saw in her rearview mirror that he watched her drive away and smiled when he waved. Strange the quick connection she felt with him. When she texted him from the hospital, he replied immediately with, *Have a great day, honey. See you tonight. Steak for dinner?*

All kinds of replies came to mind. *I'd rather eat you. Let me cook. Are you sure I'm not imposing?* But she stuck to the simplest and most honest: *Yes.*

16

WHILE GRIFFIN DIDN'T like Maeve being out of reach of his protection, the fact Dorian managed to hack into the hospital security system, allowing him to see Maeve at work—and safe—did mollify him. And, no, it wasn't stalking. He watched only in case she ran into trouble. He wouldn't put it past Antonio and his gang of hired thugs to do something drastic, like invade the hospital to snatch her.

The message they'd texted via Travis's phone —*Got the box from the doctor lady. Where should we meet?*—hadn't yielded a reply.

Had Travis lied, or did Antonio already have the fucking box? If that was the case, Maeve should be safe.

Should be wasn't good enough. Not with the dire

picture Travis had painted about Antonio's actions. While the man might not have grasped some of the more subtle details—because the Lycan bite had failed—he'd relayed enough for Griffin to know Antonio wasn't done with Griffin's city yet. How many other crooks like Travis had the fucker tried to turn? Which led to the questions, how many had succeeded in becoming Lycan, and how many had failed?

The latter was provided by Billy, who called to inform him the morgue currently held several bodies, all quarantined, given reports of the deceased going into convulsions and foaming at the mouth before dying. Bloodwork showed no drugs in their systems, and the only injury appeared to be an animal bite. Five dead in all, that they knew of thus far.

Fucking five! Just how many folks had Antonio bitten? It bothered Griffin to realize they had no idea just how large Antonio's gang might be.

At midday, the country cousins arrived with much backslapping and promises they'd scour the city for wolves. However, Ottawa wasn't a tiny hick town. Sniffing out Lycans among the uninfected human populace would be damned near impossible. Still, having them around did much to ease Griffin's mind.

While Wendell and Bernard might have a past together that left the former sour, even their accountant wouldn't deny the country boys were the best trackers to be had.

Annoying as fuck too. Griffin made the mistake of briefing them in his apartment, which led to them sniffing out Maeve's existence. His cousin Benoit started the interrogation.

"Is she hot?"

"Yes, so stay away," Griffin warned.

"Does she have a sister?" Benoit didn't give up.

"Fuck sister, how's her mother?" Cousin Baptiste, shy of thirty, liked the older ladies.

Only Basile, still married to his babies' mama, didn't join in with the ribald ribbing. He shook his head. "It's a wonder y'all have dicks left. With the way you're always fucking around, I'd have expected them to rot off."

"You're just jealous of our variety."

At that, Basile snorted. "I'll take good sex that doesn't result in a rash any day."

"I don't suppose we could get to why I called you here?" Griffin interrupted.

"Bertrand says you were shot up," Bernard stated.

With a nod, Griffin told them what had

happened thus far. He left nothing out and finished with, "This fucker is dangerous. He doesn't follow the old ways. He's using guns. He's biting folk left and fucking right. He's a menace who needs to be stopped."

Bernard nodded. "Agreed. Don't worry, me and the boys will find the bastard."

"Not just him. We need to locate everyone he's bitten."

An alert on his phone had him checking it and huffing, "Maeve's here. You all need to get going."

"What's wrong? Ashamed of your hillbilly family?" chided Benoit.

"More like I don't need you cockblocking twats scaring her off."

"Well, shit, I do believe our boy is in love." Baptiste eyed him with shock.

"And if I am?"

That led to even more rounded eyes, and then the shoving started as they tried to escape.

All but Basile.

"What the fuck is wrong with them?" Griffin asked.

"You're falling in love."

"So what if I am?"

"Those nimrods are afraid it might be contagious."

"Seriously?" The door slammed shut behind his family. He eyed Basile. "How is wanting to settle down with someone a bad thing?"

"It's not. I know that, and you're in the process of discovering that, but those twats haven't figured that out yet." Basile clapped him on the back. "Ignore them. Finding Helene was the best thing to ever happen to me. So congrats, relax and enjoy it."

"How can I enjoy it when she's in danger?" he grumbled.

"Fear not, cousin. We'll make sure no one hurts your lady."

Your lady.

His woman.

My honey.

Basile left via the secret entrance just as Maeve walked into the shop. He practically leaped down the stairs to meet her. She stood by the cash register, chatting with Wendell, who played good ol' boy for her.

"Looks like I don't need to page your beau. He's here." Wendell turned to Griffin and smirked as he caught him looking eager to see Maeve.

Her smile was worth it. "Hi."

A simple greeting, and yet, he drew her into his arms and murmured, "I missed you."

"Me too," was her shy admission.

He kissed her, a kiss that might have gone on forever if not for Wendell's cleared throat. "Get a room."

Griffin cast the older man—grinning from ear to ear—an evil eye.

Maeve actually giggled. "Sorry."

"Shall we go upstairs?" Griffin asked.

Her flushed cheeks and nod were all the reply he needed. He grabbed her bag from her, and when she protested, "I can carry it," he growled.

"You've been working hard all day. Time for you to relax."

Despite his busy day, he'd managed to have some steaks delivered, along with stuffed baked potatoes and a salad. He showed off his patio setup on the roof, replete with barbecue and propane fire bowl. She sat by it, looking content.

Fuck, he was content, cooking for his woman, asking her about her day, giving her the highlights of his, minus the stuff about Pack business.

As they ate, he regaled her with stories of his visiting cousins. She laughed, the shine in her eyes not entirely due to wine. Afterward, there was something to be said about sitting on the couch, watching *Yellowstone*—it turned out they both loved it—and snuggling. Kissing. At one point, he paused the show to get on the floor between her legs and truly show her how much he missed her.

She must have missed him, too, given she came a second time sitting on his cock while huffing his name, "Griffin."

Later, as they lay in a tangle of limbs on the couch, things got serious. "I didn't hear from the detective today. Did you?" she asked.

"I called him, actually, and he says to not worry. Bail has been denied. The guy who attacked you was wanted on a few warrants. He ain't going anywhere."

She sighed. "That's a relief. Do you think that's the end of it?"

"Depends on if they know you no longer have the box."

"I'm still trying to figure out how it was taken. I mean I took it straight from the house to work. And then the only other places I went were your shop for a few minutes and the grocery store for a few. By the time I got back home, it was gone."

"I assume you saw no signs of tampering with your car?"

She shook her head.

"Does anyone else have a key for it?"

"Brandy does." Which led to her eyes widening. "She knows about the box. I told her my father died and left me some old shit."

"You think she might have it?"

"I don't see why she'd take it."

"Would she be pissed if you asked her about it?"

"Why would she have it, though?"

Before she could text her friend, someone pounded at his door.

Maeve jumped off the couch and hunted for her strewn clothes.

Bang, bang.

He whipped a blanket from the back of a chair and handed it to her to wrap around herself. "Go upstairs. I'll handle it."

"Who is it?"

"Probably my family. Told you they were visiting."

"Oh. I'm sorry. You probably want to hang with them."

"Ha. Says someone who's never met them. Trust me, I'd rather spend time with you." He dropped a kiss on her mouth. "Go have a shower or something. I'll get rid of them and join you."

She smiled. "Don't rush. I'm jumping into that pool you call a bathtub again."

She hurried off, holding the blanket around her, and he watched until her feet were out of sight on the stairs before heading for the door and flinging it open.

Basile stumbled in, supporting Uncle Bernard. A bleeding Uncle Bernard.

"What the fuck happened?" It took everything in him not to shout. He didn't want to scare Maeve.

"I've been shot," Bernard stated before doing a face-plant.

17

Maeve eyed the tub then the stairs back down to the second floor. She had no doubt Griffin would get rid of his family to be with her. But that didn't seem right. She should head home and let them spend time—

A sharp cry had her shutting off the tub for a listen. What if Griffin was wrong and trouble had followed her here? She didn't want to meet it wearing nothing but a blanket. She headed for her bag.

She whirled as she heard the soft thud of a step. Griffin appeared at the top of the stairs, looking harried, but it was the blood on his shirt that widened her eyes.

"Are you okay? What happened?" She rushed to him and put a hand on his chest.

"I'm fine. But my uncle isn't." He rubbed a hand over his jaw. "He's been shot."

The statement rounded her mouth and filled her with questions. Later. First, she had a job to do. An oath to honor. "I'm guessing you'd rather he not go to a hospital."

"That would be preferred."

Rather than make a judgment, she became a doctor. "I'll need my medical kit from the trunk of my car. I left my keys on that table by your door," she advised as she dug through her overnight bag and grabbed some comfortable clothes.

"On it." Griffin headed down the stairs, and a moment later, barefoot in track pants and a scrub shirt, so did she, only to find herself confronting two strangers.

An older man lay on the floor, his hair a dark gray streaked with bands of pure white. A younger guy knelt beside him.

He met her gaze. "You must be Griffin's doctor friend. I'm Basile. This is my dad, Bernard."

"Call me Maeve. What happened?" she asked, heading for the kitchen sink to wash her hands.

"He was shot."

She almost rolled her eyes as she dried her hands with a paper towel. "Obviously. How many times?

Where?" She really wanted to ask who but stuck to the most pertinent details for the moment.

"*Le trou du cul* got him in the stomach. Pardon my French."

"I'd say it's understandable, given what happened." She dropped to her knees opposite Basile. He'd pulled up the other man's shirt and applied pressure on the wound.

Griffin hopefully wouldn't be long. Then again, depending on the severity, it might not matter. She didn't have a full surgical array tucked in her emergency bag.

"Let me see." She waved at Basile to remove his hand. The moment the pressure eased, the wound began to bleed—not spurting, always a good sign—the blood clean and not dirty or foul smelling, also a positive thing. She tucked a hand under his lower back to be sure before saying, "The bullet is still in him."

"It is, and it fucking hurts. Bastards using silver," huffed the injured man.

"I don't think it matters what the bullets are made of. They all hurt," she quipped. "It will have to come out."

"Do it," grunted Bernard.

"This is where I recommend we call an ambulance. They can put you on an IV, have a team waiting for you at the hospital, an OR ready."

"What are they going to do that you can't?" asked Bernard.

"Knock you out."

"Bah. 'Tis but a flesh wound."

"Papa *ce n'est pas le temps*," mumbled Basile.

"It's always a good time to quote Monty Python, and no French around the lady. It's rude," Bernard chastised his son.

"It's fine," Maeve interjected. "I understand a smattering of it, given how close we are to the Quebec border."

"Basile, grab me some of Griff's good stuff. The bottles he keeps hidden above the fridge."

"Yes, Papa." The young man—if you could call thirties young—rose and headed for the kitchen.

"I doubt the booze will hit you quick or hard enough to help," she advised, paying attention now to the wound, the bleeding sluggish. Usually a worrying sign but for the fact the injured man remained conscious and coherent.

He even managed a smile as Basile returned with a bottle in each hand.

"Ah, the bourbon." Bernard held out his hand to handle the booze himself, but Basile had to kneel and prop him up enough so he could actually drink it.

Bernard was in mid-swallow when Griffin appeared with Wendell, whom she'd met earlier that day, a much nicer man than the boy who'd been rude the day before.

Wendell's face turned pale as he saw Bernard on the floor. He quickly blustered, "What the fuck stupidity did you go and do now, Bernie?"

It was Basile who replied, "Thought he'd use his body as a shield."

"Bah. Better me being shot than the man with four kids."

Maeve eyed Griffin, who rushed her bag to her side. She pulled out a bottle of antiseptic.

"This will burn," she warned before dumping it on the wound.

Bernard grimaced. "Not the worse thing to happen to me."

"Remember that time you road-rashed your entire left side because you said it was too hot to wear leathers?" Wendell sat on the floor and caught Bernard's attention as Maeve eyed the cleaned bullet hole.

Without asking, Griffin handed her the tweezers from the bag. She poked, and Bernard sucked in a breath but still replied, "I would have made that turn if not for that stupid turtle crossing the road."

"You had an accident instead of running over a turtle?" Basile exclaimed.

"It's because I ran over the turtle I spilled," Bernard grudgingly admitted.

"Karma," Wendell stated.

"Karma was me having it as soup later."

The shock of his answer almost had Maeve dropping the bullet she'd extracted. Then again, she'd heard and seen worse. The things people did to their bodies...

"Ah, that's better. Fucking silver burns." Bernard went to sit up, and she threw herself at him.

"Lie down. We're not done."

"What do you mean not done? Bullet's out."

"I haven't stitched you up yet."

Bernard rolled his eyes. "Bah, slap a Band-Aid on it. I'll be fine."

"I see stupidity runs in your family," she muttered to Griffin, but all three men heard and chuckled.

"We're just tougher than your regular folk." Bernard winked. "Got more stamina too. But I'll bet you already know that."

That pinked her cheeks. "You really should go to a hospital, if only to have an x-ray and ultrasound done to ensure there's no internal damage."

"I'll heal just fine. Give me a comfortable bed, a

couple more slugs of that bourbon, and I will sleep like a puppy. Wake good as new."

Despite his father's protest, Basile helped the man to his feet. "Thank you, Doctor."

"Yes, thank you. Time to get back to work," Bernard declared.

"He should rest," Maeve pointed out.

"Rest is for old people," was Bernard's snorted reply.

"We *are* old," Wendell retorted.

"I'll drive him to the hotel and sit on him," Basile offered, but Wendell shook his head. "No need to draw attention. He'll come stay with me. That way, you can rejoin your brothers."

Brothers who weren't here, which made Maeve wonder where they were and what they were doing. She couldn't help but glance at Griffin, also recently shot. What had she gotten involved in?

Was it too late to get out? Movies about the mob made that seem unlikely.

"Don't want to stay with you," Bernard grumbled.

Wendell clucked like a chicken, such an unlikely sound that they all stared at him, but it was Bernard who shifted uncomfortably. And was the man blushing?

"Fine. I'll go stay in your pristine pad, because

I'm sure you're an even neater freak than before."
Bernard didn't accede gracefully.

"It might surprise you to learn I've changed."

"Oh yeah," Bernard huffed. "Bet you still do the
dishes after every meal."

As they went out the door, they could hear
Wendell rebut with, "To prevent fruit flies. Nasty
things."

Basile raked a hand through his hair. "Thank
fuck Wendell took him, because I doubt he'd have
listened to me."

Maeve saw her chance and said, "What
happened? How was he shot?"

Rather than reply, Basile shot a glance at Griffin,
who murmured, "Go see your brothers. I've got this."

Got this meaning Maeve. She crossed her arms
and glared at him as Basile left.

"What's going on?" she demanded.

"You won't like it."

"That doesn't surprise me. And how much worse
can it be? Your uncle was shot. This has to do with
me and that stupid box again, doesn't it?"

"Yes. And no." He shoved his hands into his
pockets and paced in tight circles. "It's complicated."

"Then how about you try explaining?"

"I can't."

"Because you're the mob." He didn't deny it, and

she blew out a hard breath. "Unbelievable. Finally meet a guy I can't stop thinking about, who's great in bed, and he's a bloody criminal."

"Not in the sense you're thinking. I don't go around shooting people or breaking in and terrorizing them."

"But your world intersects with people who do. And my father was a part of it." She went to the side table and the hooks, snaring her purse but not seeing her keys on the table. "Keys, please." She held out her hand.

"Honey, don't go. We can talk about this."

"And say what exactly? I don't want to be a part of whatever you're involved in. It's that simple." It wasn't actually, because it would break something inside her to walk away from a man who made her feel so good.

"It's not always like this. Actually, this is the first time things have ever been this bad. It will end soon."

"End how? With someone else shot? Dead? I'm done."

"Where will you go? You can't go home. You're still in danger."

"I'll find a place. I'm not your problem. Now, keys." She waggled her outstretched fingers.

His body tense, his movements jerky, he dropped

them into her palm. "If you need me, just text. Or call. I will come to you."

"I can take care of myself. That means no spying on me."

His lips flattened. "I would never hurt you."

"Maybe not intentionally." The soft barb had him sucking in a breath. She bit her inner cheek rather than apologize, because she didn't actually think he'd harm her. He'd been nothing but gentle. Frustrating, yes, but also kind and sweet.

The true test of his character would be if he let her walk out.

He'd better not try to force her to stay.

She went down the stairs, alone, and keyed in the code to leave the building via the door to the alley. He'd given her access immediately. No qualms about trusting her.

However, she couldn't completely trust him. He kept a secret. A big one. She refused to be that dumb woman who pretended not to see. She deserved better.

So why did her heart ache that he didn't follow, didn't say a word, just let her go? A part of her honestly had thought he'd protest.

Her car remained parked in the alley, the area around it brightly lit, a camera that saw everything aimed at it. Did he watch her? She knew he had many computers set up in his bedroom in a corner that acted as an office.

She didn't glance at the lens, mostly because her nape prickled. Someone watched. As soon as she got close enough to her car, she unlocked the door with the key fob and slid behind the wheel quickly. She clicked the button to seal the doors before starting the engine.

For some reason, she kept checking her rearview mirror as she rolled slowly to the alley exit. He didn't run out to chase her and ask her to come back.

Good riddance.

Jerk.

Luckily, Brandy had ice cream perfect for eating while dissing men.

18

"Do NOT LEAVE your post for any reason," Griffin growled into his phone at Ulric, who'd tailed Maeve as she'd left.

He couldn't blame her. She'd been thrust into a dangerous situation not of her doing, and Griffin had proved unable to shield her from it. Perhaps it was for the best that she put some distance between them, because the problem with Antonio had taken a turn for the worse.

Earlier, working off a hunch, the cousins and his uncle had gone out looking for the troublemaker from Toronto.

"You got a yellow-bellied rat in your Pack," Uncle Bernard asserted.

"My people are loyal," Griffin stated, *only to recall the one he'd just recently kicked out.*

Bernard pointed that out before he could correct himself. "Not all of them. You tossed someone out of the Pack the same day the doctor lady came here. The day she lost that box."

Griffin didn't need his uncle to draw in the rest of the lines, but he did have to wonder. "Lonnie couldn't have stolen the box, because he was the one who told her to get lost."

"And then he left the shop not long after. Did she go straight home from here?"

"No. She stopped at the grocery store up the street." Which Lonnie might have passed on his way home after being fired. Had he stolen the box?

The possibility had proved to be enough to send his country cousins looking. They'd paid a visit to Lonnie's basement apartment and found him dead—tied to a chair and tortured. They'd also found what was left of a cardboard box that had been torn apart, though enough of the label had remained to show Maeve's address. Pictures had been strewn all over, many of them stomped, a few shredded, but most intact enough that Russell, the dead Alpha in Toronto, had been recognizable.

The apartment showed signs of being searched. Drawers yanked and dumped. Mattress flipped. Properly ransacked for what?

Basile had located Lonnie's phone, and luckily

the body had remained supple enough that the thumbprint required to open it worked. Text messages had painted a damning picture. Lonnie had been conversing for months with someone he called Big Dog, going back to before he'd come to Griffin to beg for a spot in the Pack.

A plant. Spying from within.

Anger and shame burned inside Griffin, because he'd let the fucking shit in.

The most damning text, though? Big Dog had asked, *Where will your A be tonight?* Lonnie had replied immediately with the name of the bar Griffin had gone to the night he'd gotten shot. The fucker had set him up.

When that murder attempt had failed, Lonnie had tried to keep Big Dog apprised of A's whereabouts, but Griffin hadn't told anyone about Maeve.

But Lonnie had texted Big Dog about the doctor stopping in at the shop to try to see Griffin. Lonnie, in essence, had also set up the ensuing home invasion.

That hadn't been the end of it. An hour later, Lonnie once more messaged to demand Big Dog bring him all the money, because he had what Big Dog wanted. And then the idiot had waited around. It cost him his life and left a single question—had Lonnie's killers found what they were looking for?

They'd trashed his place in the search, and there was no way to know if they'd succeeded.

The cousins had picked up all the pictures but left everything else untouched, setting the stage for the cops, including a few empty bags smelling of weed. Given where he'd worked, the cops would assume an employee of a pot shop had been skimming and selling on the side. He'd lost his life in a drug deal gone bad.

Once Griffin's cousins had created the perfect cover, they'd exited the apartment, and that'd been when someone started shooting, the rifle shots sending them running for cover. Bernard had pulled a heroic-father moment, throwing himself in front of his son and getting shot in the process. While Basil had taken care of him, rushing him to Griffin, Baptiste and Benoit had gone after the shooter, as if he could outrun the two-legged wolves. They'd tackled him in an alley, knocked him out, and then waited there, knowing someone would have called the cops.

The police had done a drive-by, lights spinning but no siren, a slow ride up and down the street before turning off when they saw no one and nothing amiss.

Once the coast was clear, the cousins brought the perp to Lonnie's apartment for questioning, a questioning he wouldn't survive. He would become part of the crime scene, not only because there would be no forgiveness for what he'd done but to keep his mouth shut.

Now, the cousins were holding the perp for Griffin. Not his idea of a fun night, but with Maeve gone —and protected by a watchful Ulric—Griffin could use an outlet for his frustration. This thing with Antonio had to end.

He left his place to join his cousins.

The street appeared quiet, but he didn't park right in front of Lonnie's apartment. People tended to notice strange cars. Exiting, he had his hoodie over his head, hands shoved into his pockets, shoulders hunched. Just another dude.

Lonnie's windows were shuttered by blinds, with only a faint glow creeping through the cracks. Griffin rapped on the door twice, paused, then hit it twice more and waited.

Basile opened it. "Surprised to see you. I would have thought you'd stay with the doctor."

"Kind of hard to do, since she left me." His lips turned down at the stark admission. "Apparently, people getting shot is a line for her."

"Bah, plenty more pussy in the city," Baptiste declared from his spot crouched by the man tied to a chair. Of Lonnie, there was no sign.

173

"Who do we have here?" Griffin removed his jacket and rolled up his sleeves.

"This is Angus Gershen. Local guy. Just got out of the clink for armed robbery. Also has a few priors for domestic assault. He's a real prize."

"Better let me go, asshole. The Alpha won't like this." The man bared his teeth and smelled positively feral. A recent recruit, judging by the livid red bite mark on his arm. He'd change at the next moon if he lived to see it. He wouldn't, and the world would be a better place for it.

Griffin planted himself in front of the man. "You're right, the Alpha of this city doesn't like this one bit." He let his eyes flash to grab Angus's attention.

The man's mouth rounded. "You're one of us."

That curled Griffin's lip. "I am nothing like you and that piece of shit who sired you."

Griffin glanced at his cousins, who were sitting on the counter behind the chair, legs dangling. "I take it by the broken nose and blackening eyes he wouldn't say where Antonio's hiding?"

"You'll never find him." A smug assertion by Angus.

"Already know where the fucker is," Benoit stated. "That idiot Lonnie had the address saved on his phone. We smacked you around because you shot our papa."

"Wait, you know where Antonio is hiding?" Griffin slashed a hand. "Then why are we wasting time? Finish this, and let's go deal with Antonio."

"Yes, sir."

Griffin turned his back to the blubbering that ended abruptly. Always big and brave when they had the advantage over the weak. But as soon as they met a bigger threat, suddenly they expected the mercy they never showed.

Fuck that. There was no room in his town for pieces of shit. He was a furred crusader. A hidden vigilante. Dexter with much better hair and style.

The cousins set the stage with the new body, and when they'd finished, Griffin looked at them and said, "I'm going to smack down the ass of the fucker who thinks he can fuck with my city. Who's with me?"

Everyone, of course. Time to put an end to Antonio.

19

Brandy's tub of fudge brownie ice cream really hit the spot, but it didn't cure Maeve's heartache. Neither did the tequila, although the joint she smoked after calling in sick to work did help her to relax on Brandy's couch.

Since Maeve wasn't in the mood to deal with people, she and Brandy concocted a plan for the next day. It started with mimosas chased down with chocolate chip pancakes then marathon-watching *Bridgerton* while stuffing their faces with pizza when they got hungry.

Would food and a sweet romantic historical TV show ease her sadness? Probably not. But it was better than nothing. She missed Griffin already. A man she barely knew and who'd been nothing but trouble—and hot sex. Brandy's reaction hadn't helped once she'd been brought into the entire loop.

"*You left? Damn, girl, a sexy mobster in love is the thing we all crave.*"

"*I don't want a life of violence.*"

"*Says the woman who works amidst it every day.*"

"*Exactly,*" Maeve exclaimed.

"*I was thinking more like you're the best equipped for it. Not only will you not faint at the sight of bullet holes, you can patch them up. You could be the mob's surgeon.*" Brandy spread her hands, her expression gleeful. "*You could get it engraved on a plaque.*"

"*It's like you want me to be arrested.*"

"*Please. Most mobsters never see the inside of a jail. And as his side piece, you'd probably end somewhere tropical if the cops came too close.*"

Talking to Brandy had made Maeve wonder if she'd overreacted. Should she do a web search on mob girlfriends and wives to see what happened to them? Would that really make her feel better? She'd fallen asleep pondering and woke now to a blaring alarm.

Brandy stumbled out of her bedroom as Maeve almost fell off the couch. Okay, it wasn't *almost*. She hit the floor on her hands and knees.

"What's going on?" she grumbled, pushing upward.

A hand over Brandy's mouth didn't hid her yawn. "Fire alarm."

Duh. Blame the lingering buzz for a slow mind. Maeve sniffed. "I don't smell smoke."

"Because there probably isn't a fire. Stupid thing is always going off, which means I know the drill. We gotta go outside." Brandy shuffled to the hooks on the wall to snare a sweater.

"Why do we have to leave if there's no fire?" The thought of leaving a warm apartment for the cool night outside did not appeal.

Brandy sighed. "Because, as it was explained to me the last time I complained, maybe this time it's real, and the fire chief gets really mad when people don't evacuate. Don't ask me how I know."

"How long will we be out there?" Maeve reached for her jacket and slid her keys and phone into a pocket before slipping on her shoes.

"Depends on how busy they are. Longest we've waited is, like, thirty minutes. Usually, it's quick."

They headed out the door, joining other people in the hall, moving in the direction of the stairs. Brandy lived in an apartment building with four floors and four units per level. It made for a crowd of people on the sidewalk, hugging themselves or others as they waited. No sign of flashing lights yet.

The chill had Maeve tucking her coat closed and threading the buttons. "Hope this doesn't happen often in winter."

"Once is too many," grumbled Brandy.

Maeve shivered. "We should go wait in my car. I brought my keys." She dangled them. "We can—"

Bang, bang.

The sudden gunshots had the milling people screaming and scattering. Maeve and Brandy were no exceptions. The latter grabbed hold of Maeve's hand and yanked her down the street. The firing didn't stop, and neither did their feet. Maeve closed her ears to the shrill screams of possibly injured people. In that moment, she wasn't a doctor but a survivor. She'd do no one good if she got shot too.

She and Brandy tucked in between some buildings, panting harshly, hearts racing, afraid.

Maeve dug into her pocket for her phone, glad she'd grabbed it before coming down. She had no idea if the gunfire was related to her situation, but just in case, she could think of only one person to call for help.

Would Griffin even answer? He was probably asleep, and even if he woke at her call, would he care? She had left him.

Staring at the screen, she didn't notice someone had joined her and Brandy until he drawled, "Drop the phone, Doc."

"Who are you?" Brandy exclaimed as Maeve took a look.

Male. Twenties, maybe early thirties. Handsome, blond, stocky, and while he appeared unarmed, the guys flanking him held guns.

Maeve repeated Brandy's question. "Who are you?"

"Antonio. Your cousin from Toronto."

The claim chilled her blood, mostly because she didn't get the impression he'd sought her out for a happy family reunion. This had to be about the box. "What do you want?"

"I hate having to repeat myself, but since you're family, I'm going to ask you nicely one more time. Drop. The. Fucking. Phone." His smile held menace.

"How about I put it down gently, given I'm still paying for it?" The snarky reply emerged as Maeve knelt, her finger subtly pressing the call button before she lay it face down on the asphalt. She rose with her hands held out to show no violent intent.

"As if a cracked screen would matter. I doubt it will last five minutes once we're gone." Implying she wouldn't be leaving the alley with it.

"What do you want with me? And let me add

right now, I don't have the box." Maeve declared it before things got any uglier.

His smile held a flatness, mostly because of the coldness in his eyes. "I know you don't have it, because I last saw it with Lonnie. Fucking idiot stole it without checking to make sure the grimoire was inside. Given it wasn't, that means it remains in your possession. Hand it over, and you can live."

Maeve had no doubt he'd kill her. She didn't have what he sought, after all. "What do you mean when you say grimoire? Because the word brings to mind an old leather-bound book filled with yellowed pages of fancy script. I definitely never saw anything like that in the box."

"The outside might appear more modern and plastic, but what's within the protective cover is old and one of a kind. I want it. Where is the binder?"

The clarification had Maeve quickly saying, "I don't have it."

"But you've seen it," Antonio stated.

If she claimed she hadn't, would that make things worse? "I did. It was part of the stuff sent to me, but it disappeared when the box did."

"Don't lie. Where is it?"

"I told you, I don't know."

Antonio lifted his hand and motioned one of the

gunmen closer. "Time to remove some fingers. Shall we start with your left or right hand?"

Maeve tucked the digits behind her back. "I'm not lying. I honestly don't know where it is. Last time I saw it was the morning I put the binder and the pictures back in the box before placing it in the trunk of my car. Then I went to work. It was gone by dinner."

"Who did you give it to?"

"Nobody," she huffed. "I don't know where it is."

"Let's start with the thumb. I always find that one more satisfying than a pinkie," Antonio mused aloud.

The sheer casualness of his horrific statement almost had Maeve losing control of her bladder.

Brandy jostled Maeve aside and stood in front of her to exclaim, "She doesn't have it!"

"And how would you know?" Antonio turned his snake-eyed gaze on Brandy.

"Because I took it."

"Don't lie for me," Maeve begged. She didn't want to see her best friend hurt.

"Not lying. I really did take it from the trunk of your car."

"When?"

"At work Wednesday, while on my break. I still have your spare keys from when you loaned your car to me so I could take my mom to the doctor when my wheels were in the shop."

That explained how she'd gotten into the car, but it led to a different question. "Why?"

"Because I was curious after you told me about it." A conversation she and Brandy had over bad cafeteria coffee and stale donuts.

"Did you shred it?" Maeve asked, because she remembered thinking that might be the best option.

"Heck no. I mean it looked old, and your dad obviously thought it was important otherwise why keep it?"

"So it's still intact," Antonio butted in. "Where is it? In your apartment?"

"No. I dropped it off to someone who could translate it for Maeve."

Before Maeve could react, Antonio grabbed hold of Brandy, slamming her into the wall. He pushed his face close to hers to hiss, "Where is it?"

His intensity frightened, and for what? How could an old bunch of papers possibly be important?

"Schnape's got it. Jordan Schnape. He's a professor at the university."

Antonio didn't lessen his threatening stance. "We will go find this professor, and you will demand the return of the book, or you'll both start losing body parts. Do I make myself clear?"

Brandy bobbed her head. "No problem. I know where the prof lives. 666 Haelstrom Avenue. It's slightly out of the city. You take highway 417 and get off at Carp. Then you wanna go north to the first set of lights. Make a left. Unless you're hungry, then you'll want to stop in at the Cheshire Cat for a bite. If they're open. Which they might not be at this time of night. You really should check it out in the daytime, though, if you get a chance."

Maeve stared at her babbling friend. Fear could make a person do strange things.

The sneer on Antonio's face stung. "Get in the car. Do anything, and I will have you shot. Understood?"

Both Maeve and Brandy nodded, the latter holding her hands out and away from her body to show compliance. Maeve wore a scowl, mostly to hide her annoyance at herself. She felt dumb for leaving Griffin. She might be mad at the secrets he kept, and yet, he would have provided defense against Antonio while keeping Brandy out of trouble too.

But, no, Maeve had let some moral superiority march her right into danger. Because she sure as heck wasn't blaming Brandy for this. Antonio bore all the blame for being psychotic about wanting a stupid old book. She should have burned that box the moment she'd realized who it'd belonged to.

Brandy and Maeve were marched to a large three-row SUV. They got to sit in the middle row of seats, sandwiched between the muscle with guns.

As she huddled with Brandy on the bench seat, she wondered how her friend appeared so calm. Minutes ago, she'd not been able to stop talking.

"You okay?" Maeve whispered.

"Not really. I gotta pee so bad. And I think my tampon needs changing. You didn't bring any extra plugs, did you? Maybe some Kleenex I can stuff in my pants?" The very female-oriented spew of words had the men in the SUV tuning out, so they didn't notice when Brandy palmed the cell phone she had hidden in her sweater and showed Maeve the screen. s

20

THE RAID on the address found on Lonnie's phone proved fruitless. Antonio might be staying there, but he appeared to be out with his gang at the moment. A gang of six, according to Angus, plus a few for-hire duds, so-called because the bite hadn't worked on them.

Griffin wondered where the fucker had gone and what trouble he now caused.

He got his first hint of trouble via a text from Ulric. *Fire alarm went off in the building with your GF and her friend. Lots of people coming out.*

Griffin replied, *Stick close and keep me informed.*

Probably nothing, and yet, his gut tightened. "I need to go," he told his cousins, who rifled through the suitcase they'd found, tossing clothes left and right.

"Something wrong?" Benoit asked before sling-shotting a pair of tighty-whities.

Griffin dodged as he muttered, "I don't know. Place Maeve is staying at has a fire alarm going off."

Baptiste eyed his brothers, who then all turned to stare at Griffin. "We're all going."

Benoit added, "Might as well. Ain't fuck all here."

They piled into the two cars and headed from the airport area back to Barrhaven, where Brandy lived.

Griffin texted Ulric as Basile drove. *How are the ladies?*

No reply.

Didn't mean shit. Things were probably noisy.

His phone rang, and he answered without looking at the number. No one said hello, although he'd swear he heard voices. Someone butt-dialing? He glanced at the screen to see who, and he swore. Maeve had called but wasn't speaking. He strained to listen but heard only the murmur of voices, one of them masculine.

It roused his jealousy. He wanted to yell and let her know he was listening. But what if she'd not accidentally dialed his number? What if she'd called for help and couldn't speak? He should gauge the situation before acting on jealousy.

He pressed the phone hard against his ear, but he heard nothing now. The murmur of voices ceased, leaving only an open line. Had Maeve left her phone? Maybe she'd accidentally dropped it. He pursed his lips. He ended the call, waited thirty eternal seconds, and called back. It rang and rang before going to voicemail.

Same when repeated. Basile increased his speed. They arrived to find the flashing lights of police cruisers parked alongside a fire truck. They pulled to the curb a block away, watching.

"What happened, do you think?" Basile asked.

"I'm going to find out." Griffin swung himself out of the car and strode up the sidewalk, merging with the growing crowd as people spilled from surrounding homes to gawk at whatever was happening in their neighborhood.

Hands stuffed in his pocket, he listened and caught snippets.

"I heard, like, a hundred gunshots. It was nonstop. Probably killed dozens."

"Keep telling the wife we should move. Place ain't like it used to be."

"No one was shot. I saw the guy. He fired all the shots into the air. That broad who started screeching fell and banged up her knee. You'd think she'd never seen blood."

As Griffin neared the front of the crowd, he spotted a familiar face. He approached Ulric and muttered, "Follow."

They moved to a place where they could speak.

"What happened?" Griffin asked.

"I'm still not sure," Ulric exclaimed. "First, the alarm in the building goes off and people are coming outside. No biggie. I saw your doc lady and her friend on the sidewalk. But then someone started shooting."

"You went after the gunman." More stated than asked.

Ulric nodded. "Fucker took off in a pickup truck before I could nab him."

"Where's Maeve?" The most important question.

Ulric's expression shifted to chagrin. "I lost her. Her and the friend. They started running because of the gunshots, and by the time I looked, I couldn't find them."

The phone in Griffin's pocket buzzed. He yanked it out and almost dismissed it, given the message was from Billy. But he read it and cursed.

Brandy had texted the detective to tell him she and Maeve had been kidnapped and provided the address they were heading to.

"Come on, we've got to go."

"Where?" Ulric asked. "Did someone find them?"

"Antonio's got them. But we got lucky. We know where they're going." Now he just needed that luck to hold until he got to Maeve.

21

THE PROFESSOR's Victorian-style house on the outskirts of Stittsville, with a cupola and wraparound porch, sat on a large lot, at least an acre, if not more, making it far enough away from the neighbors that they most likely wouldn't hear any yelling.

Not that Maeve dared to try to make any noise. The guns held by Antonio's muscle made the situation dangerous.

How could this be happening? And over a bunch of old and moldy pages?

Antonio wrenched open the door and pointed his weapon at Brandy. "Go get the binder. Now, or I start removing parts of your friend."

Brandy bit her lower lip and eyed Maeve before hopping out of the SUV. Maybe she'd be smart and stay out of harm's way. Maeve should have never dragged her into this mess. Too late now.

Antonio took Brandy's spot in the SUV, putting his back to the door and watching Maeve with a smug expression that annoyed her.

Maeve couldn't help but snap, "Why are you so interested in some old book?"

"Because it's got some recipes that I need."

"Is it the secret to turn plain old rocks into gold?" she mocked.

"No, but they will make me rich. Unlike your father. He and his father before him lacked the balls to use what they had."

Her lips pressed into a line. "I have no father."

"Is what he said." Antonio chuckled at his own poor joke. "Can't blame him for pretending you didn't exist. Given the blessing can only be passed on to the son, a daughter is a waste of good seed."

"So much patriarchal, misogynist crap in one sentence."

"It's the truth. Females are only good for birthing the next generation. But apparently, Theo didn't remember that when he had the grimoire sent to you instead of passing it on to me, his closest male blood relative."

"You know, I'd have given it to you if you'd asked

nicely. You didn't need to do all this," Maeve grumbled.

"Complain, and you'll suffer the same fate as your father."

"What's that supposed to mean?" she asked, even as her heart sped up.

Antonio's lips stretched. "It means I shot the fucker and tossed him into Lake Ontario."

"You killed my father." For some reason, that made her angry, despite never meeting the man.

"He deserved it."

"Why, because he saw through you? Saw what a waste of oxygen you are?"

"Keep insulting me and see how that goes for you."

Maeve knew she courted death, and yet, she couldn't stop. Why not ask all the questions? At least then she'd die with some of the answers.

"Are you still part of the Toronto mob Theo Russell was in charge of?" She couldn't call him *my father*.

"Mob?" He laughed. "Such a human thing to say."

"Meaning what, that you don't think you're human?" She eyed him and wondered what fantasy he'd concocted in his mind. Apparently, one where an old book was worth killing for.

"I began life like you, but my father was special, and he passed on that greatness to me. But did my uncle recognize it? No. He refused to elevate me to a proper position. Wouldn't let us move into the twenty-first century. Thought he could lead the Pack forever."

"So you killed him, proving he was right." Maeve shook her head. "You are unfit."

His eyes tightened to slits, his lips flattened, and menace oozed. She thought he would shoot her, but instead, he glanced past her, glaring at the house through the windshield. "What's taking her so long?"

"It's only been a few minutes," Maeve argued, knowing she had to stall for time.

"It shouldn't take long to find one book. Maybe your friendship doesn't mean that much to her." He aimed his gun at her head.

"Or the professor is being difficult about returning it. If it's that rare, he might be trying to claim some kind of privilege over it." Maeve had no idea if that was even a thing, but Antonio apparently thought it might be.

He waved his gun. "Get out. You're coming with me. We're all going inside."

Maeve couldn't decide if that was a good thing or not. On the one hand, she needed to give the detective time to arrive. On the other, if they were inside, would it be harder for the cops to rescue hostages?

In the end, she had no choice. All four men got out of the SUV with her and Antonio. He ordered two of them to stay outside and warn him if anyone approached. The men in the other two SUVs remained where they were. He took a pair inside with them. No knocking. They just kicked open the door and stormed the house as if they were some kind of elite task force.

They weren't—even Maeve could spot they were sloppy. They had no idea how to sweep rooms. They went stomping and yelling through the first-floor rooms, only to end up in the vestibule to report back to Antonio, who'd remained there with Maeve.

"No one here, Alpha," said one guy, pockmarked and too young to yet realize crime didn't pay.

"Check upstairs," Antonio grumbled.

Off the men went, splitting at the top of the staircase to hit what were surely more than a few bedrooms. Minutes passed.

Maeve stood there, trying to not draw attention to herself. Where was Detective Gruff? Surely he should have arrived by now.

Antonio wandered to the foot of the stairs and yelled up, "Pascale?" No reply. "Gofer? Any of you fuckers?" Not a single person replied to his query.

He returned to Maeve's side, snapping, "Exactly who is this Schnape?"

She shrugged. "No idea. Never met or heard of him. You'd have to ask Brandy." Who'd also disappeared.

Thump.

Both their heads tilted back as they glanced at the ceiling.

The noise Antonio uttered made him sound more like an animal than a man. "This is a trap."

He shoved Maeve away from him, and she hit the edge of a table then the wall, snapping her head hard. Dazed, she leaned on the table and blinked at the sight of Antonio lifting a gun in her direction. If he fired, she wouldn't be able to avoid the bullet.

"Think you're so much better than me. You're lucky I still need you."

Antonio grabbed hold of her hair and dragged her to the door. "Fucking whore. As bad as your father." With a hard yank, he tossed her through the door, where she stumbled and fell down the three steps to the graveled drive.

"What's up, boss?" asked one of the guys waiting for them.

"Company. Get everyone out of the trucks," Antonio ordered, gesturing to the parked vehicles.

"Locked and loaded. Shoot to kill anyone in that house."

No. It was more a horrified thought than an actual exclamation. Maeve pushed up on her hands and knees, knowing she had to do something. And then she ducked as a furry blur soared out of the house, the four-legged body slamming into Antonio and taking him to the ground beside her.

It took a moment for her to grasp what she saw— a wolf trying to eat Antonio's face, its jaw snapping and throat rumbling.

Antonio held it out of reach and grunted. "You're supposed to be dead."

An odd thing to say before they rolled away from Maeve, who blinked and then had to do so again, because Antonio had disappeared. Now two wolves wrestled.

Wolves.

She needed to get away from here. And find a hospital to get treated for the hallucinations caused by her injuries. She pushed to her knees as a car skidded into the driveway behind the parked SUVs. The two vehicles disgorged guys armed with guns. Along with the two already outside, she counted nine shooters against whoever was in that one car, which suddenly spun into reverse, its tires throwing gravel as the driver tried to get out of range of the gunfire.

The cracking of weapons kicked Maeve into survival gear. Instinct screamed she needed to take cover. She crawled, grunting and huffing, only there was nowhere to hide, as the shooters went from aiming at the car to aiming at the fighting wolves.

"Get the gray one," someone yelled.

A yelp sounded, and the gray wolf that had leaped from the house slumped to the ground, sides heaving, bleeding from a wound. The other wolf snarled over it. It wouldn't be long before it turned its malevolent glare on her.

She needed to find cover. Inside the truck would work. If the keys were in the ignition, she might even be able to escape.

Her grip on the door handle froze at the snarl behind her. She whirled to see the wolf stalking toward her, done with the limp pile of fur on the ground behind it.

Detective Gruff hadn't arrived, and men closed in, laughing and waving their guns, oddly howling.

"Bite 'er!"

"Rip her to shreds!"

They all had something to yell, none of it good for her.

They were distracted enough that they didn't

realize a speeding car approached, its lights turned off, until it was too late. Many of them turned just as it struck.

Chaos erupted as the men who hadn't been hit took aim with their guns. She had no time to watch the battle as the wolf continued to stalk her, head low, snarling. It coiled on its haunches to spring.

"Don't you fucking touch her!" Griffin's voice emerged clearly as the gunshots cut off suddenly, along with the fading scream of someone dying.

The wolf didn't turn its head. It leaped, and that was when Maeve knew she had a concussion, because Griffin also lunged. Only, it wasn't Griffin but a wolf that slammed into the attacking lupine. They hit the ground hard and tussled.

Wolf Antonio and wolf Griffin.

Not real. She pressed her body hard into the SUV at her back, as if its very solid nature could bring back reality.

Nope. She must have hit her head harder than she'd thought, because wolves fought in front of her, wrestling and tearing at each other.

Her leg throbbed, and she looked down to see it soaked in blood. She'd been shot. How could she not have noticed?

As blood spurted, it occurred to her that she really should apply pressure. Her fingers slid in the warm wetness. She slumped to the ground, her ass hitting hard enough to jolt her entire body. Her head tilted to the side, her eyelids heavy. Signs she was losing too much blood.

A hot huff of air momentarily widened her gaze. A pair of familiar eyes set in a furry face peered back.

"Not real," she muttered. She let her lids shut and sighed in relief as, instead of hearing a woof or feeling a bite, she heard Griffin say, "Don't worry, honey. I've got you."

He caught her as she fell into darkness.

22

GRIFFIN HELD Maeve's unconscious body and had a complete and utter mind fart.

What to do? She'd been shot because he'd not been there to protect her. What if she died?

It took a woman snapping her fingers in his face and yelling, "Snap the fuck out of it. Maeve needs help."

Griffin stared at the curvy woman with very curly hair as he said dumbly, "You're her friend Brandy."

"I am. And you must be that handsome guy she's been yapping about."

"She talks about me?" He couldn't help his surprise.

"Too much. Although I can see why. Nice body.

Does the mob always fight naked?" she asked as she tore at Maeve's pants, exposing the wound.

Her remark reminded him of his nudity. Seeing Maeve in danger, he'd shifted quickly. "She's hurt." He glanced down at Maeve's pale face, doing his best to ignore the blood—her blood—scenting the air.

"Looks like the bullet went through clean. In and out. Messy. Painful. But we can get her fixed up as soon as we get her to a hospital."

"She wouldn't need fixing if someone had protected her." The low growl drew Griffin's gaze. With a scrap of Antonio's shirt around his hips, a big man pointed at Griffin in accusation.

Griffin recognized the man. "You're supposed to be dead."

"Don't fucking change the subject." Theo Russell, the not-so-dead Alpha, glared.

"I'm allowed to be surprised," Griffin snarled back.

"Is it really that surprising, given how dumb my nephew is? As dumb as you are."

"Don't blame me for your mess. My town was problem-free until you and your nephew caused trouble."

"What's your excuse for defiling my daughter?" Theo snapped.

"She's a grown woman."

"She's my daughter."

"Not according to her."

"Don't you fucking argue with me, boy," Theo uttered in a low threatening tone.

Griffin scowled right back.

Brandy intervened. "Fight about it later. We need to get Maeve to a hospital. Like, now. She needs a transfusion."

"She can have my blood." Theo held out his arm.

"You're kidding, right?" Brandy snorted. "You'll probably need one, too, given you've got just as big of a hole."

Theo glanced at his own oozing wound. "Bah, it's just a scratch."

For some reason, Griffin almost laughed. He'd said the same not long ago.

"Even if you hadn't leaked a bunch of blood, I wouldn't use you, because even if you are family, I don't know that your blood is compatible."

"It is. She's my daughter."

Brandy shook her head. "Okay, fine, but how do I know your blood is clean?"

"It is."

"I don't have the proper equipment." Brandy threw out another excuse.

"Schnape does."

"You're being awfully insistent." She pursed her

lips. "I'm assuming you want to avoid the hospital because going there would draw unwanted attention. Making this a mob thing."

Theo's brows lifted, but so did the corner of his lips. "You are correct."

"Okay, then, let's get her inside. Somewhere flat to lie on. Dining room table should work."

"I'll go warn Schnape and get him to pull out the field kit," Theo offered.

"Find some pants while you're at it. I shouldn't be looking at my BFF's dad's and boyfriend's dongs," Brandy yelled. Then, in an aside to Griffin, who rose with Maeve in his arms, she said, "No offense. I'm sure your dong is very nice, but you're Maeve's man."

"I don't know if she'd agree."

"Because she thinks you'll get her into trouble. Which I hope you will. She's been way too serious all her life. She could use a little shaking up. And a werewolf is just the thing."

He stumbled but didn't lose hold of Maeve. "Um, what?"

"Don't even try to pretend you and her dad aren't wolves. I've read more paranormal romance than you can imagine, and I know the signs. The wolves fighting followed by naked men all over really gave it away."

He winced. "You can't talk about it." Maeve wouldn't like him if he had to kill her best friend.

"I won't, on one condition."

He almost feared asking. "What?"

"Don't break my girl's heart."

"I'll do my best." He lay Maeve gently on the dining room table and then stepped back, accepting the offer of pants from Ulric, who'd never lost his to start with. Only Alphas could shift outside of a full moon. Griffin hadn't wanted Maeve to learn about him in such a violent fashion, but when he'd needed to move fast, he'd had no choice. Only the wolf could give him the speed to counter Antonio.

The fight with Antonio hadn't lasted long. No wonder the fucker had chosen to usually fight with a gun. He'd lacked the strength and skill of a true Alpha, even if he had been able to shift at will.

"Is that really her dad?" Brandy asked Griffin as she returned from the kitchen with damp and dry paper towels.

"Yeah."

"Wonder why he's finally doing something about Maeve."

"Probably because his supposed death started the snowball of trouble."

"It all comes back to the box or, more specifically, that binder she inherited." Brandy swiped at Maeve's leg, who flinched and shivered even as her eyes remained closed.

He stood by her head and stroked her temple, feeling useless. The others of his Pack, including Billy, were outside, rounding up Antonio's posse, who'd lost interest in fighting once their boss had died. Ulric acted as a nurse, handing clean paper towels to Brandy, who applied pressure to the wound.

Theo returned, wearing pants and a sweater, alongside a bespectacled gent with a plastic bin marked Medical. Theo and Griffin held Maeve down as Schnape poured antiseptic on her wound.

"Owww!" Maeve sat up suddenly, screaming. Griffin managed to steady her. Maeve stared into the face of her father and whispered, "Daddy?"

Her eyes rolled back, and her body went limp, but Griffin held her so she didn't fall.

Brandy sucked in her lower lip. "Think she'll stay out long enough for me to stitch?"

"Give her blood first." Theo held out his arm. Schnape held tubing.

"Are you sure you're a match?"

"Don't argue. Just do it," Theo barked.

"Could you maybe say please?"

"Don't push me, considering I've yet to decide if you should live."

Brandy blinked. Griffin interjected, "Ignore him. Nothing will happen to you, because you're under my protection. Please, help Maeve."

"Don't blame me if this doesn't work," she muttered. Brandy ran a line from Theo to Maeve and then went to work stitching the wound. Maeve remained unconscious the entire time.

By the time she finished, Brandy appeared quite pleased with herself. "And this is why nurses deserve more responsibility. Ain't only doctors who can fix things."

"Thank you," Theo said.

"Don't thank me yet. Now we see if you were right about the blood."

"It will work."

"Is she going to start howling at the moon and chasing cats?"

"You tread on thin ice, young lady," Theo chastised.

"Calm yourself, FILF. I'm not telling anyone about your secret."

Theo blinked. "FILF?"

Ulric leaned in to whisper, and the older fellow actually blushed.

It might have been funny if Griffin hadn't been so concerned. He carefully climbed onto the table so he could cradle Maeve to his body, drawing Theo's attention. Brandy left for the kitchen with Ulric, meaning they were alone.

"How did you get involved with my girl?" Theo demanded, arms crossed over his chest.

"Blame Antonio. He shot me, thinking if I died, he could take over my Pack."

"Dumb fuck. I told my brother he didn't have the right temperament to be wolf."

"What was in that box that he wanted so badly?" he asked.

"A collection of old recipes."

"What kind of recipes?"

"The kind that would be very dangerous to our kind if they got into the wrong hands."

"And you didn't burn them?" an incredulous Griffin asked.

Theo shrugged. "Didn't seem right. What if they were needed someday?"

"Why leave them to Maeve, though? Shouldn't they have gone to someone who would have understood what they were?"

"I wasn't expecting everyone to think I'd been killed, and my guess is Robert believed I had been, which was why he sent the box to Maeve, along with the letter and pics."

"Why did you pretend to be dead for so long?"

"I didn't. Getting shot and tossed in a river kind

of sucks, especially when you wash ashore and don't remember right away who you are. Once I did, I returned to Toronto to discover Robert was dead and Antonio missing, along with the binder."

"But how did you know to come here?"

"The recipes are written in a very old and specific French dialect that can only be translated by a handful of people. The most likely one, given his proximity to the city, was my old friend Schnape."

"What if you'd guessed wrong?"

"Knowing Antonio, all Lycans would have been fucked." Theo hung his head.

"What are you going to do now?"

The big man shrugged. "Guess I'll go back to my Pack and resume control."

"I meant about Maeve."

The man appeared pained as he said, "I know she hates me for leaving, and I can't blame her."

"So that's it? You're going to walk away?"

"What else would you suggest?" the man hissed.

"Seems to me like you've got a second chance. Up to you what you do with it."

"Maybe." Theo appeared thoughtful as Brandy reappeared.

Griffin had some questions. "How do you know Schnape? Why did you bring the book to him?"

"When I was in university, I took one of classes

on how languages evolve over time. I failed but he was super nice about it. Since the writing on those pages Maeve inherited reminded me of French, I figured if anyone could translate it, he could."

"Your meddling could have had dire consequence," Theo warned.

"Actually, seems like my meddling is what saved everyone's life so feel free to send me a fruit basket of thanks." Brandy didn't cow at all under the alpha's glare. "That's enough blood out of you. Don't need your ornery ass croaking." She severed the blood connection between father and daughter, but Maeve remained unconscious.

Theo flexed his hand and rose. "I should go before she wakes."

"Are you sure?" It wasn't Griffin who asked this time but Brandy.

"She's going to have enough to deal with today without adding me to the mix." The man grimaced. "Take care of her, or else, boy."

"I plan to."

Theo offered a curt nod before heading off into the kitchen. Brandy pointed at Griffin. "Professor says you can borrow a bedroom for the night. I'd suggest the first one to the left at the top of the stairs. It has its own bathroom."

"Thanks." He carefully lifted Maeve and took

her to a bedroom that could have graced any mansion from a hundred-plus years ago. Brass bed frame. Quilted cover. He snuggled Maeve under the thick layers of bedclothes as she started to shiver. Having not dressed yet, he simply slid in with her, cradling her body against his.

He woke to her softly murmured, "Griffin, is that you?"

23

MAEVE DREAMED she was in some kind of Grimms' fairy tale with monsters. How else to explain the vicious fight between wolves, one of whom had Griffin's eyes?

As if he were a beast.

When she woke, disorientation led to her freezing in fear for a moment as she found herself in someone's arms. She relaxed as soon as she realized who held her.

Griffin.

Brandy must have called him after everything had gone down. Her memories were kind of muddled. Her wolf dream mixed with reality to fill in some of the dead spots. It made it hard to know fact from fiction.

"Hey, honey." He nuzzled her hair.

She tried to shift and winced. "Ow. What happened?"

"You were shot."

"I vaguely recall that." She reached down to run her fingers over a bandage. "How come I'm not in a hospital?"

He stiffened. "It was a clean shot, and we had supplies. Brandy stitched you up."

Meaning they'd not wanted to have the police involved, a fact that bothered her. "What happened? I'm kind of fuzzy. I know there was a guy, my cousin or something. He wanted the binder from the box."

"That would be Antonio. He was the one behind all the attacks."

"What happened to him? My memories are messed up. I remember gunshots, and for some reason, there were wolves. Which is nuts. Happened right before I passed out."

"Antonio was handled. As was his gang. You don't have to worry about them anymore."

She didn't ask if he'd killed them. Having met them, she'd discovered a savage side to herself that thought *good riddance.* "I guess you got my phone call."

"I did, but I couldn't hear a thing."

"Then how did you know where to find me?"

"Billy told me." At her puzzled look, he added, "You know him as Detective Gruff."

"You mean the cops are in on the mob business too?"

His lips twisted. "Just one. And not the mob. At least not anymore. I wasn't lying when I said I went legit. Unfortunately, some people are still trying to do things off the books and illegally. They force us into situations we don't want."

"If that's true, then why not call the police to deal with it?"

"Have you seen the bureaucratic mess that is our legal system? Sometimes it's quicker and simpler to handle stuff ourselves."

"Vigilante justice."

"Yes. Which I understand might be too much for you."

"You wearing a cape and pretending to be some kind of superhero would be too much."

"Does that mean I can wear tights?"

"Only if you shave first."

He chuckled. "Or I could be the kind of vigilante that doesn't need a costume. Maybe I'm a secret werewolf."

She laughed. "As if a werewolf would choose Ottawa as his home. Now your cousins... I could believe it of them. They've got a wild, untamed vibe about them."

"Are you saying I'm not ferocious?"

"You are, but more like a cuddly bear kind of scary."

"A bear?" He stared at her.

She nodded. "Which would explain your love of honey."

"Only one honey," he growled before taking her into his arms.

EPILOGUE

MAEVE'S INJURY healed with a scar that Griffin kissed pretty much daily. Easy to do, given they lived together.

When they'd left the professor's house, minus the binder, which they'd locked in a safe, Griffin had refused to take her home.

"I am not letting you out of my sight."

It meant being pampered, which she didn't mind. She'd been taking care of herself and others for so long it proved a pleasant change.

Life settled into a routine that didn't involve thugs intimidating her or a crazy cousin out for blood. She never saw or heard from Antonio or his gang again, nor did the police ever come knocking to ask about the altercation.

Life was good—make that incredible—once Maeve chose to ignore the fact that she had fallen in love with a legit drug dealer and had moved into his home above a pot shop. To recover from her gunshot injury, she took time off from the hospital, which had turned into a resignation. Not because she didn't want to help heal but so she could follow her dream to open her own family practice clinic. There was a shortage of those in the government-funded system. While she wouldn't take money from Griffin, she did however let him look over the lease for an office nearby that she easily converted. It was within walking distance of their home, no driving involved. Since she didn't need her place, she rented it to Brandy, who came to work with her at the clinic.

A month after the shooting, she'd never been happier. She looked forward to finishing work each day and going home to Griffin.

Now, she had only one more patient before she shut the clinic for the day and went to see what kind of dinner surprise he'd concocted.

Brandy entered and dropped the new patient sheet on her desk. "Don't shit a brick when you see the name."

Maeve almost shat a brick. Theodore Russell. Seeing her dead father's name took her aback. Then again, it shouldn't have, given it wasn't an uncommon first or last name.

"Good thing I know he's dead, or I'd be freaking," she joked.

Brandy didn't. Unusual. Instead, her friend said, "Listen to what he has to say."

Before she could ask her to explain, a man filled the doorframe.

Maeve's jaw dropped. "You're supposed to be dead."

Her father shrugged and offered a sheepish smile. "So I keep hearing. And I know you'd probably prefer it, and yet, I'm here. Hi, I'm your shitty excuse for a dad." He held out his hand. Not asking forgiveness nor groveling.

It would be easy to hold a grudge. Maeve took the extended hand and shook it. "I'm the amazing daughter you shouldn't have abandoned."

He nodded. "I know that now. I made some mistakes, an especially big one when it came to my involvement with you. If it's all right with you, I'd like that to change."

"Let me guess. Almost dying gave you a new perspective."

"Actually, you almost dying is what did it."

"How did you know... Never mind." Griffin had

most likely told him, given the two men knew each other. "Aren't you worried I won't like you?"

"A chance I'm willing to take." A smile ghosted his lips.

"I won't call you Dad."

"That's okay. But expect me to brag about my daughter. A doctor. Your grandmother will love that."

That caused her to blink. "I have a grandmother?"

He nodded. "And an uncle. Two cousins who aren't psychopaths. Oh, and my sister, who will probably skin you if you call her aunt. She likes to pretend she stopped aging at twenty-nine."

Family. Huh. What a concept after so much time alone. Her mother hadn't had much contact with her own family, and when she'd died, Maeve had thought that was the end of any family for her.

"Would you like to come to dinner?" Maeve suddenly asked. "My partner is making steaks for dinner. I could get him to thaw an extra one."

"I would like nothing more."

Despite herself, Maeve liked the man she refused to call Father. But she loved the one who didn't bat an eye when she brought home a mobster from another city.

Griffin offered her father a beer, gave her a kiss,

and whispered, "Your father said if I don't make an honest woman of you, he'll kill me and dump me in the Ottawa River."

"And what did you reply?"

"That I've already bought the ring and was waiting for the right time to ask."

He hit the floor on one knee and held up an open box. His lips crooked as he said, "Honey, will you—"

She answered with a kiss.

BRANDY WOKE PASTY-MOUTHED, in her bed that for some reason, she shared with a massive dog. Last thing she remembered was partying at Maeve's wedding dinner. The wine flowed freely along with tequila shooters. A lot of them, which Brandy kept downing. However, her recollection of things after dessert was served got a little hazy.

Apparently, she'd hit an animal shelter and adopted another pet. The big lump of fur didn't move at all when she shoved out from under its heavy paw.

At least she still wore her dress and panties, meaning she hadn't gotten too freaky. Still, a wolfish looking dog in her bed? Good thing it wasn't a full moon, or she'd have assumed something else. The Lycan thing had been explained to her by Ulric and Quinn. According to them, non-alphas required a moon to shift.

I wonder what possessed me to adopt a dog, though? Especially once as massive as this one.

To her surprise, when she stood, she noticed Froufrou, her kitten, sleeping tucked against the massive beast. A good sign? Or the calm before the wolfdog made her kitty its snack?

A visit to the bathroom left her bladder empty and when she emerged—her wrinkled dress stripped in a favor of a long, voluminous robe—the wolfdog had disappeared. In its place, a naked man sprawled across her bed. And a nice one at that.

Bleary eyes opened and widened at the sight of her.

"Good morning!" she chirped. "Although, it would be better with some coffee, and Tylenol. It seems I had a few too many last night because I don't remember anything after the crème brule, although given I was cuddling a wolf when I woke, I'm going to assume we did it doggy style." A joke, but how did he respond?

"I gotta go." The naked hunk literally dove off the bed and bolted from her bedroom.

He'd be back. After all, he lacked pants and even

if he did manage to escape, Brandy knew where Detective Billy Gruff worked.

GET READY FOR THE NEXT FURRY ADVENTURE IN BIG, BAD GRUFF.

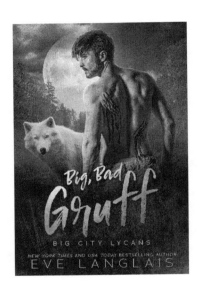

For more books and fun see EveLanglais.com

Made in United States
Orlando, FL
14 January 2023

28681684R00124